TIGER WOLF

—

(a novel in ¾ time)

BRIEN COLE

ETT IMPRINT

Exile Bay

To Malenka

First published by ETT Imprint, Exile in 2019. Reprinted 2019.

ISBN 978-1-925706-85-7 (paper)
ISBN 978-1-925706-83-3 (ebook)

Cover painting by Brien Cole
Cover design by Robyn Oliver
Book designed by Hanna Gotlieb

Wolves howling,
All in chorus
An evening of snow

Josu

In a Distant Time.

In blue bathing togs on a Lake Zakopane shore Joseph Klein was seven years and two months. He was in a whizz. Bird egg rocks dappled and spotted to overturn, to flick, rock to rock, or wave to wave, a rock tiled beach punctuated by black basalt causeways. The wind was chill, it blew off the waves, the waves a noisy green. Joseph's father, yelled at Joseph, to wait, not run, as lake-ward as he was. He stopped and waited at the high water of periwinkles. There, the basalt was smooth but scratched, the same sharp scratches as an ice-chest floor. Joseph announced to an astonished father. "The Zapopane was once a lake of ice." At that moment Joseph discovered the world, by this he meant the natural world, hitherto composed of mysteries, was capable of solutions. His father pronounced the word, "Geomorphology," a word which belonged to the ancient ice. His father prophesied, a dazzling career for Joseph at the Jagiellonian University, Krakow, if ever he was to grow stronger by the waters. Every summer, every autumn, every spring to lake Zakopane they came for the waters, with the Tatra mountains green as green or gold and yellow or covered in snow, and once in winter, he saw the last wild wolf pack on a lake's distant shore.

Another century saw another land, Joseph Klein became a naturalist, explorer. The century, the twentieth, the land, Tasmania, the exploration of its high Western Tiers. Here, also the ice had carved its will. A high plateau inclined on an angle. Joseph calculated in nineteen twenty eight, to be eleven degrees, falling north west to south east. A land of lakes and lakey ground, frozen in winter, squelching in summer, of heath and fen and occasional copses of native pine. Joseph collected data. Every fact dispels a mystery. One by one, all the mysteries of the world will vanish beneath the microscope and theodolite. Joseph Klein believed this for fifty-two years, until he saw the first photograph of Birkenau.

An old man, nearly blind, began that Birkenau afternoon, another study, once again he used the word geomorphology, for want of another. No longer would he study the landforms of the world, his would be the geomorphology of the psyche, by this he meant the narrow world of those people who enter his study. His son Eugene, Jon's son Paul, Paul's wife Genevieve, their first son Jeremy and second son Nathanial, the strange boy with the flashlight.

And naturally, the ghosts, his son Jon, his father who visits him now quite regularly to chat, his mother, to sit embroidering with her weak eyesight and his wife Naomi. It interested Joseph little the individual psyche, the geology, he described it of mankind. No, his study was, as it is in Genesis, the bedding down, generation to generation, the upheaval of youth, the lattices of marriages made, the progeny, and progeny of progeny. "The psyche", he concluded in his lucid hours, "is just as subtle, but not quite as old as the land upon which it dwells."

PART 1.

In The Year of The White Wolf

Hobart Mercury March 1972
Lake Pedder is not a walk in the Park!

A government minister has warned walkers against venturing into the South West Region of Tasmania as protesters plan to gather on Lake Pedder shores for the final time. Weather conditions in the Lake Pedder region can deteriorate quickly, the Lake Pedder track would become a quagmire and visibility in the region would be reduced to zero.

In what has been dubbed the "Pedder Pilgrimage" walkers will spend this Easter converging on Lake Pedder for the last time, in spite of mounting concern from the Hydro Electricity Commission. The Hydro (H.E.C.) maintains its primary concern is for the material development of Tasmania. The future power needs of the state can only be met by the construction of this dam. "Anything else is simple sentimentality," a H.E.C. spokesman stated, adding "There have been no significant protests against the damming of Lake Pedder." The Tasmanian Premier has dismissed all the submissions made by the conservationists, and fully backs the authority of the H.E.C.

1. Cartography

Eugene Klein had not thought about his father's expeditions to the great Western Tiers, had not thought about the South West of Tasmania, nor his families place within it from the December he had sailed for England and war to the December when Martin McKenzie and Jan Lizbeth had knocked his Museum of Victoria office door open to invite him on, "a bit of a jaunt."

"Down to Tasmania, one last time to the Lake."

The walking community was in a fizz. The magazine of the Melbourne Trampers Club, had written an obituary to "the death of Lake Pedder, a gem of the south."

Eugene had never been there, he was only the man with the maps.

Eugene Klein cartographer, a maker of maps, a maker and collector for if his father Joseph thought that the profound push and pull of the bedrock defined our being, Eugene was content with the contour of surface. Oh! He understood the limitation of the craft, Eugene understood that a line is not a river, a contour not a peak. Flight Officer Eugene Klein navigated Lancaster bombers over the Austrian Alps in 1943 he understood, the lines on the paper won't kill us but Mount Zuckerhuti will, a map, even your own map is only ever an approximation.

He lent Martin McKenzie and Jan Lizbeth the maps they would need. He didn't join them. He wished he had. Lake Pedder was a gem of the south and now it is lost. And from that day he started thinking again of his father's many expeditions to the Tiers, of the war and of Nadia, he took out the photo's the maps and the tears. It was probably the reason that his grand-nephew began to draw on his graph paper pictures of him standing next to the bomber of Cambridgeshire fields.

2. In which Nat meets Rosalind.

At the age of fourteen Nat Klein had invented projection. He invented it the moment he turned his birthday flashlight beam on through his birthday magnifying glass, the moment he lent over to kiss his dying Great Grandfather, who had whispered, "Just a little longer, just wait a little longer and we will see the wolf pack on Zakopane shore." Such that Nat simultaneously discovered the first law of optics; the first law of the psyche; that at least in his family, reality will always be an act of will. No other day in his life would ever seem so full. Not the day he invented the reel, the second invention in his very private and confidential book of inventions, nor the day he first linked his two-inch-wide wax-paper cartoon panels into a moving, living cinematography. Nor the day in which, in Derwent pencil, number thirty-one, cobalt blue, the drew for the first time the cloak of his hero, "the Green Avenger." Nor this Saturday, in the beginning of the year, which will become, the year of the white wolf. In the Victorian Museum, in the gallery called progress, when he met the girl in whom he would discover love. Her name is Rosalind Son-Lee. She is drawing the bones of the anthropoids with her best friend Elizabeth Kylie.

Rosalind is a Chinese Australian, she stands only as tall as Nat's upper lip, her hair is cut in a bob and she wears tortoise shell glasses. She stares intensely at the glass caged anthropoid bones and draws meticulously. Nat would have liked to tell her to hold her drawing hand less stiffly. Her drawing is too stilted. Nat is watching Rosalind from where he sits, copying the details of a locomotive R766, which features in his cartoon. Elizabeth watches Nat. Nat watches Rosalind. Elizabeth walks towards Nat. She has a very assured walk, she is blond and brown, a robust outdoor brown.

"You draw well," Elizabeth says, "is it for school? My friend Rosalind is drawing the cave man for school."

"It's a kind of cartoon," Nat answers.

Rosalind walks over to stand behind Elizabeth. She watches Nat draw. She has a habit of twisting her right hand around her left index finger as if it were a dial, it is a habit she will keep for ever and the first day they met was the first time Nat noticed it.

"It is a cartoon." Elizabeth tells Rosalind.

"It is actually only the design for a cartoon, the cartoon is in my Great Uncles office, in the South West Wing."

Nat hesitates. He doesn't want to say too much. He doesn't want to blab, when he is nervous he either says nothing or he blabs. He is nervous now. He doesn't count on Elizabeth. Elizabeth wants to know everything. Rosalind confirms Elizabeth's sweeping request. "It is true", she speaks precisely, "my friend has an insatiable curiosity. Elizabeth wants to be a T.V journalist, she likes to interview everyone."

Nat began by telling the two girls that his uncle (Great Uncle) works in the museum as a cartographer.

"That is a map maker."

"Really", says Rosalind, in her most condescending manner.

Nat hesitates again, boy, do smart girls make him nervous. He neither wishes to have Rosalind look at him again as if he is a complete idiot or tell them the complete history of his family, which would confirm it. The everything Elizabeth wants to know, and which Nat is hesitant to explain, is exactly that, a disjoined family history.

A family history told by a nearly sixteen-year-old cartoonist, is Rosalind and Elizabeth will discover, a history founded on images and myths, inexplicably linked to the South West wing of the Victorian Museum, the repertory of Nat's mythology. Here, (in fact Eugene's office) where Nat found the photograph of the leather clad flight crew standing before their Lancaster Bomber, the photo which begins his cartoon, Uncle Eugene third from the left. Eugene with those forties' matinee looks, striking, dark and handsome, dashing in his RAF moustache, which he still sports although it's grey and Eugene faded with it. Nat has something of his looks according to the family, and in reality, it was here, where Nat found the black silk jacket from the far eastern exhibition of nineteen twenty-eight which he knew to be the Green Avengers. And the leather flying cap which he wears while he draws, he knew to be his own. Neither Rosalind nor Elizabeth would of course, ever be able to separate reality from illusion within the south west wing, nor Nat ever wish them too. He wishes only that they become the first people he will guide into the south west wings storage rooms, to whom he will tell of his Great Grandfather's parade of exhibitions to that distant and difficult land called the Great Western Tiers. The first people to learn what his family knew of that early twentieth century naturalist and explorer, of the moment in a distant childhood when he found ice scratches on a lake Zakopane shore or saw wild wolves bounding distant and wee.

The first people to learn of his first and least known exhibition to the Tasmanian Tiers when Joseph had carried a gramophone but no sextant and travelled in exhilarating circles, dazzled by the gigantic glaciated land he could not place in the world, circling to the ceaseless sound of his beloved Chopin mazurkas. Of subsequent exhibitions in which he mapped the landscape, measured its fall of snow, its breadth of ice, its colonies of heath and pine.

He tells them of the animal which he found on the Tiers, similar but not identical to the European wolf, yet a wolf all the same, in its strong compact frame, its fierce canine jaw, the pattern of its hunt. Joseph gave it a name *Thylacine alpine*, and tried in vain, to have it recognized by the zoological department of this very museum. "It is now," he admits, "considered a fraud."

He tells them, indeed shows them, how in the menagerie, which is the south west wing storage rooms, a person can find many things some of which have been labelled and some of which not, therefore free, forever to be imagined. These are the things which Nat re-assembles to create his cartoon; the silk cloak the Green Arrow wears, the mysterious calligraphy of his head scarf, the bleak black garments of the Seventh Samurai, a leather cap, a Zorro king of mask and the bombardiers large steel plate with its hinged transparent grid folding over which is the perfect cartoonists tool to square every frame and the action within. The small black shadow puppets from the far eastern exhibition which have become the stencils for his characters, the heroic Green Avenger and the villainous Seventh Samurai.

Naturally he cannot tell them this without Elizabeth nagging him, "show us, the place where you sit and draw, show us the flying cap you wear while drawing on your fighter pilots' seat." And finally, "show us, the entire seven metres of wax-paper drawings sped through your home-made projector.

The projector is the first invention in Nat's private book of inventions. It's not, he thinks, his best invention, but the only one that's ever worked. Mark Three, the one he's now using, has exchanged his Great Grandpa's glasses with a beautiful tortoise shell magnifying glass, his thirteenth birthday present from his brother Jeremy, the cardboard shoe-box projector frame with a wooden box painted jet-black. Nat has drawn a cartoon seven meters long in which the Green Avenger has trailed for twelve thousand kilometres the seventh and final Samurai of the Rising Sun.

It begins with the title, "The Adventures of the Green Avenger" in bright red texta, then follows the credits.

Director Nat Klein.

Producer Nat Klein.

Scriptwriter Nat Klein.

Animater Nat Klein.

Music Nat Klein.

There is no music. (He hadn't wanted to ask his musical brother.) The first scene, over which the opening credits are flashed is the still photograph of an aircrew beside the Lancaster Bomber on Cherry Hinton Fields, Cambridgeshire. It is a photograph of his Great Uncle, third from the left clad in leather. His Uncle is the navigator. Squad leader Hugh Hennessey is the pilot, there are two gunners a co-pilot and the mysterious Green Avenger. They take off, flying over the channel. Nat has drawn a minute speck of aircraft against a massive backdrop of cloud.

"Bad weather over Belgium." Hugh Hennessey says above the racket of motors, ack-ack flack and rumbling of the "old bus" pitching into a storm.

The action cuts to a map of Europe, a thin red line representing the aircraft as it crosses the Belgium coast, the Rhine, and into Germany. They will fly via Salzburg, the River Enns, the Austrian Alps. The scene cuts again, inside the fuselage. The navigator taps the Green Avenger loosely on the shoulder, pointing to the fluorescent hands of his American wristwatch, seventeen minutes, he points with eerie enthusiasm into the quarter moonlight and scattered cloud. There is no sound, words spoken are written in balloons like an old silent movie. It ends abruptly for it is, of course, incomplete.

Nat must tell them how the Green Avenger will parachute into a picture postcard village somewhere in the Dolomite Alps, how he will make his pursuit on the Vienna Express. He was drawing the replica of the engine in the hall called Progress when they met, and how many things, many wonderful, dazzling things some of which he, the creator, cannot yet know will happen, for that is the nature of heroic adventure. It must be full of mystery and romance.

"Do you like Nat ?" Liz asks Rosalind once they've left, "he likes you", she lied . She'd told the same lie to Nat, "You know Rosalind likes you." She giggled.

3. In which Rosalind discovers a wolf.

Four days later at precisely seven forty-five p.m. Rosalind Son-Lee rings Nat to ask, if he'll be in the Museum this Saturday afternoon, she was thinking of going, of finishing her drawing, and if it happened, he was there, could they meet over coffee.

"You will be there of course."

"Why, yes, of course I will." He answers and immediately wonders why. He'd never, ever met a girl before, not like this, not like a date. And Nat doesn't even drink coffee.

Nat's parents are in the dining room, where he has been watching them from the stairs above the telephone stool. They have cleared the dishes to one side of the dining room table and are drinking there, "after the children have left the table" coffee. They are having a loud discussion, some loud discussions are like arguments, and this loud discussion is particularly like an argument. The subject is "the study," and "Eugene", the study which was once Great Grandpas and is now accepted by all but Nat's mother as Eugene's. Nat's mother would like Great Grandpa's study for Jeremy and her music room. Nat's mother would like Eugene to clean it out, would like Eugene, as she says to "pull his weight" and spend less time side-tracking Nat, or "that boy will amount to nothing" like Eugene, she inferred but didn't say. Great Grandpa's study is still cluttered with debris from another century and another land, and even in a house as large and as rambling as this, "a room," Nat's mother observes, "is still a room, and that room is ideal for Jeremys music room."

It is also ideal for Nat and Eugene to sit and talk and dream of dazzling expeditions to wondrous unknown lands. There is in fact no better room since this one contains so many mementos of Josephs lifelong travels. {Many but not all, for a proportion was donated to the Museum of Victoria as the Klein bequest.} Neither Nat nor Eugene want what has always been unofficially their room to be given to Jeremy. Although only Eugene is aware of its inevitability, for Nat is about to grow up. He and Nat to grow apart. The world as always to turn. Nat is more aware of the chance of finding something wonderful in any sorting out of Grandpas study than he is the inevitability of the world turning.

Paul {Nat's Dad} says reluctantly, "Yes , it is time it was done."

Nat's father is embarrassed by everything which Nat finds exhilarating, his Grandfather's exhibitions, the wolf, of course it is a fraud, and the time his Grandfather spent, away from his family the sign of a purely selfish man.

As Genevieve {Nat's Mum} yells, "Nat can you take these dishes out." When everyone knows it's Jeremys turn, but that is just how it is.

Eugene does not need to be told, the world has turned, the time has come, he begins on Saturday afternoon, while Nat has coffee with Rosalind Son-Lee. Rosalind sat, oh so self-assured and sipped the coffee which tasted bitter. And Nat was as nervous as nervous can be, wondering, if this means something silly, like they are girlfriend and boyfriend. While Eugene opened reluctantly; the first draw of his father's desk, the first box of his father's legacy.

Eugene was hesitant.

Eugene was nervous.

He didn't know what he might find. Eugene, the vaguely ignored second son, was as much concerned that he would find something about himself as he was that he would find nothing, that is his father's eyes he barely existed.

In the first draw he finds; postcards from Leipzig, letters from Krakow, Deeds and Diplomas, a military exception dated nineteen nineteen.

In the second locked draw he finds, papers in the process of writing, unfinished notes on that strange distant landscape, certificates of birth, certificates of marriage.

In the locked glass cabinet tied in red and white ribbons {the colours of Poland}; he finds his father's diaries.

In the second locked cabinet he finds the charts, and mounted on sheet after sheet of pasteboard, pressed plants of fen and heath.

Eugene simply began by emptying draw after draw onto the study floor, then stacking everything into one of five piles placed strategically around the room. He thought of many criteria for naming the piles in a scientific manner and chose finally; journals, journeys, love, letters, and litigation. Into litigation he places whatever bears the stamp of the world's institutions. These he deals with first, all Saturday afternoon while Nat met for the second time the girl in whom he would discover love.

Rosalind Son-Lee sits in the fighter pilots seat wearing Nat's leather flying cap and goggles as she doodles on his cartoon clipboard.

She says, "I've been thinking of those trees, the ones your character, what's his name, the Green something, will descend into, once he jumps from the plane, parachutes from the plane, sorry. There is a photograph you could use to base your drawings on, it's one of my parents, who had their honeymoon in the Dolomites Alps, very near the Green Avengers drop-site."

He hadn't expected Rosalind to remember that, it surprises and pleases him. He says, "Yes, I'd like to see it."

Then he tells her today, Eugene has begun to explore his Great Grandfather's study. She wants to know everything, she emphasises, "everything."

"Whatever you find, for you cannot tell with science, what might be a clue. You know to the mystery of the wolf. You think it's a mystery, don't you Nat? I like to think of science as a giant Agatha Christie mystery. So, if he finds anything, anything at all Nat, will you tell me?"

He promises he will. They shake on it. He crosses his heart and hopes to die.

"I'm glad I came today, I'm glad I rang, it's good to talk to someone else from a scientific family."

Rosalind's father he has discovered is a Professor of Chemistry, and Chemistry is, very definitely, her very best subject. He smiles, that kind of smile which says, I'm glad I met you too .

Later in the evening Nat walks Rosalind to the Camberwell tram. She is quiet. She is often quiet. It is because she says, "I don't want to waste time talking about mundane things." Sometimes, she thinks mundane things, the mundane thing she is thinking now slightly embarrasses her, for it is, "When will I see you again?" But as she crumbles her ticket through the Kew Junction barley a mile from leaving Nat, she wishes that silly girl away.

Eugene has dispensed with litigation and has moved to the pile labelled, "letters". He has built a large wooden frame, the year written along the top of the frame, and the source of the letter down the side. The letters are held in place with three hundred and seventy-eight alligator clips, and three hundred and seventy-eight nails.

Letter number one is underneath the date December ten, nineteen-o-eight. This letter is written in Polish, the language of Joseph's childhood and the second language of Eugene's. It is from Joseph to his mother.

Dear Mummy,

It snowed last night. The snow was blue. Yesterday I heard a wolf howl. Do wolves kill you Mummy? Daddy says they do. Tomorrow I'm going to see the wolf again. Daddy says we will.

> *Love Joseph.*

Mother to son, son to mother these letters form a single unbroken pulse for forty-seven years.

There are letters from Arlo Levi pharmacist and friend discussing always provisions and practicalities. Letters from Colin Bradshaw, photographer and sometime biographer; letters to the Museum of Victoria; letters to Dr Karl Vonoski, early mentor and friend. Eugene translated Polish to English. His Polish is rusty. His German is worse. He let German be, he had he considered trouble enough with Polish. Forty-seven years of letters, mother to son and all of them talking about how it is, you know son, down the street, in the market, where merchants of Warsaw, are surely the worst pirates a lady will meet.

A small thing like coffee, how the prices have risen! Eugene began to graph the price of coffee from the day of his birth, the twenty third of August nineteen twenty-three. The price of coffee on that day was a high seventy-five zlotys per kilogram. Eugene isn't sure what a zloty is worth, whether it is a coin or a note? Perhaps it is a lot to pay for her kilo of coffee. He isn't sure. He entered school, and the price had near doubled, one hundred and six zlotys, would you believe. On the day, so long ago now, when Eugene accompanied Joseph on the final expedition to the Great Western Tiers, {during the spring, "Let me see it must be, nineteen thirty-three, when he was so young."} The price of coffee had topped one hundred and ten.

What an adventure! The first of his life; to journey with his father into a snow-covered world of mountains and glaciers, or so he thought then, ice lakes for skating and heathlands beneath a crust of long icicles, plastered by wind. It was then that he saw it, a glimpse of the wolf, however uncertain because of the mist, between pine wood forests on a lakes distant shore.

He kissed a girl and the price had quadrupled. Her name was Kathline Rankin and she had straw blond hair.

He entered Melbourne Grammar {the school he went to; Paul went to and Nat goes to} with the price of coffee at six hundred and one, Melbourne University with the price at eight hundred.

He would never know how much his grandmother had to pay for her one kilogram of coffee in the year nineteen forty-three when Eugene's Lancaster bomber let its payload of thousand-pound bombs fall on the western borders of his father's homeland. Although he knew, they all knew, not necessarily then, that their Jewish Grandmother could not possibly have survived, and didn't. He would never mention to his father how he flew his bomber low over the villages of Poland. How, one by one, night by night, the names of his father's childhood were lost beneath a cloud of white explosion which boomed beneath his wings. When Eugene left for the war, he left a father, vigorous of argument, striking of appearance, when he returned he met an ancient figure, a man of contemplation who was only able to explain his transformation with the words. "Poland is a dream, played by Chopin."

Nat sits on a foot ladder, helping Eugene, neglecting his studies, reading the letters, written in English as he clips them in their order by year and person. He finds nothing to interest the girl, who on Tuesday, sends him the photo she'd told him about.

A small, black and white snapshot of a women standing on a precipice above a forest of hazy grey pines. Written on the back, in the neatest of printing, "Miriam in the Austrian Alps, November sixty-seven." Miriam is Rosalind's mothers name, it is a strange name for someone who looks so Celtic, Miriam Son-Lee. She has amber hair and a pale northern face, she looks not the slightest like her daughter, who has written a note.

"The trees are a local fir , the altitude fifteen hundred metres, the rock predominantly dolomite. If the Green Avenger descended here twenty-five years prior, snow would have covered the Kara pass into Austria". She has added, as an aside, "My parents would often climb here during my father's time in Cavernish, Cambridge. It is incidentally why they named me Rosalind, after Rosalind Franklin, a Cambridge girl (whose fate I will not emulate.)"

Nat copies this photo onto a wax-paper transparency, minus Rosalind's mother, into this transparency the Green Avenger will descend through fifteen frames of drawings.

The second time Rosalind rang, once again at precisely, seven forty-seven, Nat has little to report. His uncle has found nothing about the wolf, and little of the expeditions, all that must be in the journals for it is not in the letters and not in the notes. Uncle Eugene has not begun on the journals yet and may not for some time.

"Gene is actually a very meticulous man."

"Then we must begin on the journals."

They must begin after school. They'll rendezvous at the Junction, at three fifty-four. They'll cut down the train lines through Frog Hollow Reserve, sneak into Nat's room, by four seventeen. Lie on the floor, between Nat's bed and the wall and untie the red ribbons around the first stack of journals.

The first entry is dated the year nineteen twenty three. The first words are in Hebrew. Nat recognizes the word mountain and the name Krakow. Then follows a passage written in German which Rosalind translates with difficulty in her best schoolgirl way. Much English, some Polish, a French phrase and Russian, written in three alphabets, "four", if you're Rosalind for she counts the Greek letters Alpha and Omega.

The journal entries read something like this. "August the fifteenth, nineteen twenty three, a scattered mist on Lake Sidon banks." Then in Josephs meticulous notation, the following facts.

Ambient Temperature	5 Degrees C.
Ground Temperature	3 Degrees C.
Wind Direction	South-south-west.
Wind Speed	5 Knots.
Wind Chill	2 Degrees C.
Visibility	Marginal.
Precipitation.	
As Rain	Zero.
As Snow	5 mm.
Water Temperature	1 Degree C.
Depth of Ice	10 cm.
Percentage	
Ice Cover	17 Percent.

Every day the same climatic data, familiar camp details and the business of exploration. August the sixteenth dawns frost sharp, as Rosalind whispers.

"It's so very real Nat, it's like it is happening, you can sit back, imagine that we are both there. I feel cold already." She says with a shiver, as she moves even closer, touching his knees, with thin brown girls' legs.

"It's like a cartoon, before someone's drawn it. It's so very visual, so very real." Nat re-ties the ribbon around the first of the journals giving Rosalind the second of the nineteen twenty three. He will smuggle back the first and return with a drawing pad, onto which Rosalind can write clearly the scientific data. Average temperature, and snowfall, for each day and each week. Average wind speed, direction, cloud cover above them. The coldest of mornings and the warmest of days.

For how many weeks were the lakes iced up completely?

For how many months did the snow cover the ground?

When Rosalind has written all these facts onto paper, after she has twisted her little finger about, after she has bitten the end of her pencil and taken her glasses away from her eyes. Squinted at Nat, likes girls in the movies, pointed out how his Great Grandfather had spiralled, in vast doubtful circles, exploring this land, minus a sextant but complete with a gramophone, he covered the country to the bars of a waltz. What could she say to sum up the data but three words which left them unsure where to go.

"Interesting, but incomplete."

And asks Nat again, when next they will meet.

He says, "on Tuesday, can you get away, a little bit early, skip class about three."

She supposes she might do, but, "where shall I go."

"Meet me at the corner of Little Latrobe, there is a door in the basement, it leads into the Museum, the staff only section. Don't worry, no one will see us. I use it a lot."

"Okay," she says touching his shoulders, squinting and smiling in a school-girlish way.

All Sunday while Nat drew the Green Avenger descending onto the photo that Rosalind had sent, he wonders just how having a girlfriend begins. How can you know what a girl has been thinking? How can you know if a girl wants to kiss? What is it like if you do it? Is it covered in spit? He wonders, uncomfortable thoughts about kissing. Will they have to get married? Will they have to elope?

The answers to these questions his brother will know. He'll have to ask Jeremy when they lie in the dark.

"Jeremy," he asks him, "You know how it is. How girls sometimes make you think, that they want you to kiss. Well what if you've nervous? If they slap you the way, they will do in movies. Well how do you know?"

Jeremy lies on the top bunk and stares, up at the ceiling, it's just what he does, when he is thinking of music, or thinking of girls. He is not quick to answer, because he likes to think more than his brother ever would or could. He contemplates the question with a knowing kind of smile. "There are three types of girls Nat, I will answer all three; noisy girls are the easiest you don't need to know, they will kiss you if you don't, they don't like to wait. Then there are shy girls, they will never let you know, but they will stand very close Nat and shy girls don't slap, and then there is the mysterious, I'd keep away from those, you can't ever tell what they're gunna do."

All girls are mysterious when your only fifteen and nine months, when you're crumbling your tram ticket after skipping from school. After you've tucked your school uniform into your Grammar school bag, and hoping a prefect isn't catching this tram. Nat arrives a little early at three minutes to two. Five minutes before Rosalind who is so rarely late.

Eugene is bustling all over the place. In a frenzy of motion from basement to roof. He had an idea in the middle of lunch, nearly choked on his sandwich, it was so flaming good. He'll map out the journals on a vast sheet of wood. It might explain lots of problems he's having right now, like how could his father be two spots at once.

"Look here! In the journals," He shows them to Nat, "he says quite distinctly, he's supposed to be here {On the side of a mountain, cliffs down to a lake} whereas in his letters he claims to be there {at Lake Sidon camp}. My father hadn't wings as far as I know, so something's not right here and I want to know what. I've discovered a way to map both at a time. I've invented the first, map that maps truth, or lies if you like. Each fact has a colour depending on proof. It is exactly the map I need for my dad, in brown I've drawn places and red I've drawn camps."

The map is enormous. It fills up a room, with shades of each colour from deep red to pink, from the blackest of browns to one almost white, a feather of colour like a mist on the ground. There are deep blues and light blues and all sorts of greens, a most wonderful map, whatever it means. The place it is mapping is many miles across, it's a large block of land pushed up on one edge. That edge is all mountains, which are rocky and rough. The mountains are steep if you approach from the west but rise so gently if you come from the east, like the top of a table that's covered in lakes, a vast misty table where Joseph was lost for so many weeks as he journeyed in arcs. These journey's just smudges, the palest of pinks, like a gramophone record they sweep around lakes. Other places are certain Eugene's marked them in black; Mersey Crag and Mount Zion, he knows where these are, Mount Jerusalem also and King David's Peak, others are less so, the New Year's Lake, a Lagoon that is mentioned in one of his notes and the second of Tiers, is probably not.

He can't wait to show Rosalind, she'd love to see this.

"Rosalind!" yells Nat and races away, down the steps, through the galleries, "I've forgotten about Rosalind, I hope she's still there."

"Where on earth have you been?" Rosalind's fuming at Nat.

"Eugene is making a most wonderful map, come on, let's see it, quickly, this way."

He leaves Rosalind behind him as he scampers along, through mazes of doorways some of which say, "No entry," in red letters but Nat just ploughs through. Rosalind follows and hopes they aren't caught by someone official, she hates being in trouble, being in strife. Nat knows the Museum better than most, they are soon in the map room where Nat's Uncle Eugene is way, way up on a ladder, painting a dot.

"The map is a wonder but not quite the point, I cannot see on it the sighting of wolves."

Rosalind sits down on a ladder, takes a journal to read; September the seventeenth nineteen twenty three.

Rosalind translated from German a long-passed evening surrounded by snow, snowed in at Lake Sidon, the weather is poor, the explorers are grumbling with little to do.

September the eighteenth, a lull in the storms, allows a reconnaissance up to the Tiers, but little reported except low cloud and snow, they collect weather data and quickly return.

September the nineteenth, the weather turns bad, the temperature plummeting in advance of the wind.

Everyone is just waiting for the blizzards abate, it's not much fun sitting curled up in your tent.

September twenty ditto, twenty-one just the same, but clearing by noon enough for a note, pencilled in along the margin, an incidental remark, "the wolves are about us on the lakes distant shore."

"So here," she whispers, "it begins."

4. Eugene's three wishes.

Ever since Rosalind was eight years old she has recognized her destiny to solve the world's mysteries via microscope and test-tube, to wear a white lab smock and peer through dense glasses at columns of fingers on a neat grey clip board. Rosalind Son-lee, scientist, that's what she will be, yet until she'd met Nat there were no mysteries to solve. Her first is the wolf, and Rosalind will solve it, she swears that she will, she will not let anything get in her way.

Ever since Eugene was twelve years old he recognized his destiny was to be a maker of maps. Maps are more than an adventure from a well cushioned chair, maps are more than a landscape neatly bound within books, you scroll with your fingers through unknown terrain, maps are a world far safer than there, far warmer and drier and closer to home. Maps are a means to make sense of the world, to strip out the detail until the patterns are left. If you get lost in the detail, you get found in the map.

Eugene recognized his destiny, the day he began, drawing the landscape in the Lake Zakopane snow-jar, the snow jaw which once served as his father's paperweight and now serves as his. A wonderful snow-jar of houses, pines, lake, a land he imagined far greater than was. He drew steep rising contours of foot-hills and mountains, peaks with sharp summits and cliffs never climbed, glaciers, rivers and lakes filling valleys. He drew villages whose centres were steep spired churches, fronting cobble-stone squares. He drew railways which zigzagged up conical mountains, snow tipped, and shrouded by misty grey cloud. He drew whole cities whose river ambled beneath bridges, broad tree lined avenues, gardens and squares. A wonderful map of land full of beauty, it took him a month and seventeen colours and when it was finished all his father could say, was.

"When the railway leaves Krakow, how high does it climb to, arrive at the station on Lake Zakopane shore?"

"Is this too steep to ask of a railway or have you invented a new kind of track?"

"If there was an atlas of lands kids have imagined on what page do you think your glorious map should be entered, in the pages called magic or the pages called home?"

Very few conversations between Eugene and Joseph had ever been this long, although every conversation between them was always quiz and answer, answer and quiz. And no, a steam locomotive could not have climbed his line, Krakow to Lake Zakopane, but yes, it was a map of both, for Eugene it was magic for Joseph it was home. The reason Eugene Klein remembered this rather than any other conversation is that it was the closest Joseph ever came to praising him. Eugene Klein became a cartographer. His father did not praise him again. Never again did he use the word "glorious" to anything Eugene Klein accomplished. Twelve years later Eugene unfurled a real map of Southern Poland in the fuselage of his Lancaster, thirty thousand feet over the Reich land, with a payload of ten thousand-pound incendiary bombs. He unfurled it, then rolled it back up again. He wouldn't need a map of Southern Poland to drop this damn payload on the cities and railways of his childhood vision. He remembered each bearing to that glorious land, the longitude and latitude of every railway and factory. He directed his pilot and blew them away.

Everyday Eugene watches Nat drawing the frames of the cartoon he's calling, "The New Adventures of the Green Avenger". It is a wonderful cartoon, what he has seen of it so far, he's drawn it so playfully, so vibrant and whimsical, but Paul hasn't told him, that he thinks it is grand.

"If Nat was my son," Eugene begins to think thoughts which don't really help him, don't help him at all.

"If I had a genie, and three wishes to wish. The first of my wishes would be to convince Nat's father to be a better father than my Dad or his."

The second wish, he thought about ever so long, was to do something, anything, completely his own, not just draw maps for other people's projects, but do something which only Eugene Klein can do.

The third wish is simple, he has wished it for years, to see; for an hour, a minute, a day, but see her just once, before he is dead, the girl who he dreams of each day since she left, like so many parted by the directives of war. He just wants to see her, it's as simple as that. He just wants to see, his Nadia Kaminski again. Nadia, the heroine who Nat Klein draws, will meet up with his hero on Dolomite pass. Unlike Nathanial, who makes up tales, wonderful, wonderful tales, but tales nevertheless. Eugene knew Nadia. He knew her arms, they held him. He knew her touch, a tingling, soft unease. He knew her lips, fierce lips. In the year of the photo taken in Cherry Milton Fields, Cambridgeshire, Flight Officer Eugene Klein had flown seventeen missions over the Reich land and had known Nadia Kaminski for ten months. Nadia would not have been at that drop site that night, she was with him in Cambridge, but yes, she was very beautiful and very brave, and Eugene was terrified, every moment, every day, every night raid, in every way. Some people weren't, he will never know why, Nadia was one of the wasn't.

Nat Klein would not have known what to say to his father if he had told him his drawings were great. He had no other ideas of what a father ought to be that catch the tram at eight type-father he had. He would not have known how to deal with the first of Eugene's wishes coming true, nor perhaps with the second, but knew he could deal with the third, for Nat has wished that same wish, it is only to be expected, since Nadia will meet his enigmatic hero as he floats down to earth.

"Adventure," huffs Rosalind in the tram to the junction, "what more adventure does anyone need than the quest for the wolf?"

"The Thylacine is a fraud."

"You don't know that Nat."

"Do you?"

"No, but I'm going to ask tons and tons of questions until I find out."

Rosalind Son-Lee neither knew what those questions may be or to whom those questions should be posed. Plainly, not to Nat who ought to be helping but is wasting his time drawing silly adventures, which aren't based on facts. He ought to be helping unravel the clues, since it's to do with his family, he ought to know more. He ought to at least know just where to begin, at the very beginning seems the best place to start.

At the very beginning of the mystery of wolves, were two easy questions, the first, too simple for words, for a girl whose best subjects are biology and chemistry. This question is; what kind of animal is a wolf?

The second more important question is, in what kind of landscape will it be found?

Rosalind asks Nat to try and remember anything, anything at all that his Great Grandfather may have said, about the Thylacine, about the land, about the exhibitions, and about his life. She asks him as the tram rattles along Riverside drive.

"I was too young when my Great Grandfather died. He told me some stories but so long ago. It's Eugene who might know something more of the wolf. You see, he has seen it, when he was a child."

"The Thylacine"

"Yes. Or so my mother says, for there are many things my Uncle will not talk about and that is one, the war, of course, is the other."

"If only we could ask him."

"I don't think anyone ever has."

5. The Girl whose souls an Express Train.

Nadia did.

"Would it be snowing?" Nadia had asked. She thought it dazzling, so wonderfully dazzling to discover a wolf.

"Tell me more," she said, "I must see it, I must close my eyes and see it."

"Was it snowing?" she'd repeated.

"Lightly", he'd answered.

"Was the snow soft, was it flaky, did it melt in my hair or could I brush it away?"

Nadia Kaminski had the most beautiful, beautiful hair, copper and frazzled and when the snow touched it, it'd glint like a jewel.

"It was flaky, it melted as you touched it."

"Was the snow I was standing in crusty or slushy, if the snow was flaky perhaps it was slushy, but I must not presume. Tell me Gene what was it like?"

"It had been icy in the morning, it was no longer icy but not yet slushy, it crunched underfoot."

"Was it cold?"

My father said it wasn't cold, my father said it was like springtime in Krakow, but I found it cold."

"This is a wonderful secret Gene"

He told her of the low pines dusted with snow, the pandanus which he explained looked a little like a giant green bottle washer, of the mist hanging very low, so low the ridge which you knew rose high before you were just, or just not, a different shade of whiteness. The lake he told her was frozen but not enough to skate on even at the edges where the ice was thickest. You must break the ice to fetch water from the lake.

"Is that when I saw the wolves?" she'd asked.

"Not yet, you don't think it is your turn to fetch water, your boots are wet, and your feet are frozen, but you dawdle at the ice because it isn't your turn and it isn't fair." It was, of course, Jon's turn.

"Do I brood or am I angry. I would be angry, but you would brood, and I must remember I am borrowing your eyes." She smiled faintly as she said that without opening her eyes.

He tells her she can see it now, something moving at the edge of the pines were the ridge begins to rise steeply for the valley is glaciated.

"What colour is it?"

"It is a very light tan, but it has stripes like a tiger on its rump."

"I see them now Gene", she'd said, "There are two of them and the male is leading, they are bounding up the spree, which is covered in snow like a table-cloth. They are having fun Gene."

She laughed, then smiled, then laughed again. Later as she lay coiling her long legs over Gene's she'd asked, "How many compartments has the soul?"

"Does the soul have compartments?" he'd queried.

"Oh yes." she was adamant. "the soul is an express train; but I don't know how many compartments I have left, tonight I have filled one compartment with your wolf, and one I had already filled with your love."

She smiled one final time the smile of a sparkler.

What Eugene told Nadia, he incorporated into his enormous map, and eventually into the model of the map, the first model a simple three-dimensional relief map of the tiers. It didn't stay simple, (whatever does). It started to grow. It started to grow into the place he'd told Nadia about, such that, if Nadia walked into the model, she would walk again into that moment.

He could only hope, she might smile again.

Nat Klein both knew and did not know Nadia Kaminski. He knew the family legend of Eugene's one great love. He knew the photo he found between the pages 151 and 152 of the book, "Climbing in Britain "was her. And he knew it was the face of his heroine, with a heroine's alight eyes, a heroines richly ruffled hair and the striking square cheek bones of a heroine's face. The very first time Nat saw the photo of the face of Nadia he knew she was the woman the Green Avenger would meet as his parachute crumbles into the pines of a Dolomite drop-site. What he did not know is how deeply, insatiably in love, the Green Avenger would be with Nadia.

"You awake Jeremy?" Nat had asked in the bedroom dark the night he found the photo.

"Why?"

"Do you think there are girls who have never been kissed, whose faces are so beautiful if you touched them they would break?"

"It's not very likely, but perhaps it could happen."

"I think the Green Avenger has fallen in love."

"Go to sleep Nat."

"I think he has fallen in love with that kind of girl."

He fell in love with her the very first time he saw her.

The very first time Eugene Klein saw the face of Nadia Kaminski, the war, his war, was seven raids old, and Eugene fell in love too.

February nineteen forty-three, on Cambridge banks, a wolfhound barking caused Eugene to turn, to meet eye to eye a lean, dark and very handsome women dressed in a W.R.A.F. uniform and a silver scarf, who called to her dog, "Minsky come here"in the dialect of Krakow.

He said in much the same dialect, imitating his father, "Your dog is disrespectful."

"He has a free spirit." she answered in English.

And because she had a free spirit she asked him to walk with her and talk to her in his amusing Polish. They crossed the bridge of Sighs, crossed St. Johns courtyard, passed before the Cavanish buildings. (Where Dr Son

Lee would one day meet Rosalind Franklin) The wolfhound bounded ahead. Nadia paid it little heed.

"The dog," she said, "is more attached to me than I to her, therefore she will not stray."

She smiled, and her smile began to unsettle Eugene, for it was both unusually beautiful, like a sparkler, and unusually nervous, like a sparkler. She took his arm as they walked the "Backs" and said in her most wistful Polish,

"It's so extraordinary fragile Gene, every moment."

From that extraordinarily fragile moment Eugene Klein's soul was derailed forever.

Nadia was lost in the confusion of war and Eugene returned to Melbourne, never to marry, to work as a cartographer in the Victorian Museum, to live in the family house and watch it pass through generations of better, abler and elder sons, and hope one day the yearnings would subside. They didn't.

If he had three wishes the last one would be to see for a minute, an hour, a day, the girl who had told him her soul was an express train.

The war changed Eugene, the family decided, without ever understanding why. Naturally their friends agreed; the war changed everybody.

Eugene Klein flew thirty-seven missions over the German Reich, beating the odds of surviving by twenty-one missions. He was lucky, everyone said he was lucky. Squad Leader Colin Ramsay, said he was lucky, he was certainly luckier than Colin, who died over Dresden. Luckier than bombardier Syd Colby, luckier than Hugh Hennessey, they were lost over Poland. He was lucky to survive, lucky to come home, to suburban Melbourne, 33 Fordham Ave, a nice neat brick veneer house, double story with garage room for one Austin. Eugene Klein did not doubt, all things considered, he was lucky. It was however a funny kind of luck, an empty kind of luck. When Eugene Klein returned from the war, he had stopped feeling terrified, he had stopped feeling devastated, by the loss of Nadia. He felt obliged to feel joy, he felt obliged to feel as lucky as he was told he was. Instead he felt nothing, nothing at all. And while elder brother Jon came back from his war, the Pacific War, and took up his interrupted life. Eugene could not.

Nothing would ever be the same again and he wished a forth and most peculiar wish to do something as exciting as war, without the noise and the bloodshed, something his own. That something he began to see was the map, the model of the map, of the place he'd once described to Nadia, the place where he saw the wolf.

It was he thought a wonderful idea to build a model of the place he had mapped. To see the vast, graduated map of his father, turn into a landscape of lakes and of mountains. A model constructed on a scale unequalled, an entire gallery will be taken up with the Great Western Tiers. No model so big, no model so wondrous has ever been built in the Victorian Museum.

The way he conceived it a viewer would enter through a pencil-pine forest, over a ridge made of fibreglass rising from via steps from the pencil-pine forest to heath banks and ice.

Once in the model they will glimpse that cold landscape, the land he told Nadia of, so many years ago. A land of ice lakes, ice mountains and rivers where he once glimpsed an animal, of which no-one believes.

PART 2.

From The Journal of the White Wolf

Melbourne Age November 1982
Not another Pedder

The Federal Government will not intervene with the Tasmanian Government's proposal for the Gordon below Franklin dam. A spokesman for the Tasmanian H.E.C. stated that the dam is necessary to guarantee the future power needs of the state. To which the premier agreed, "I think it is a common sense decision."

The Australian Heritage Commission says a moratorium should be imposed immediately on construction and an environmental study undertaken. A proposal the H.E.C. rejects, siting all statuary requirements have already been fulfilled. "The claims of the conservationist," it states, "are insubstantial."

6. In which Eugene finds a blizzard.

Martin McKenzie (lake Pedder Martin) knocks an ajar workshop door open, raises thick eyebrows on an otherwise bald head and thrusting forward an enormous, muscular arm, re-introduces himself, to Eugene.

"Martin McKenzie, mathematician."

Martin McKenzie, mathematician wears an Edinburgh University tie, pinned with a tie clip which paraphrases Gödel's proposition V1. "All theorems fall apart in the wash."

He swivels a stool up to the wall of Eugene's enormous map. He, a tall man, is dwarfed by the lines of varying blue along the Great Pine Tier. He runs a finger around the glaciated, royal blue shore of Lake Sidon.

"What kind of pressure does it take to gorge that?"

He must know the answer for he doesn't wait for Eugene to give one before turning abruptly towards a startled Eugene Klein.

"The rumour is, you are after ice."

The rumour is all over the Museum. The rumour says, Eugene Klein is about to submit an exhibition featuring the mythical *Thylacine alpina*. Of the fifty-five staff of the Victorian Museum, fifty-three have heard the rumour, and fifty-two of those who had heard it considered the plan; "lunacy, stupid, ridiculous, mad." The one who didn't stood before Eugene Klein with.

He says, "A wonderful idea."

But first Eugene must follow him to the place most appropriate to explain. That place exists not far away at all, in fact only a fire escape away, the top of a fire escape away, on the tar black roof of the Victorian Museum.

He coaxes Eugene up onto the roof. "Where the air," he says, "is so blissfully clear".

Here he draws, on the black-tar roof, a one-inch square in startling white chalk.

"A solar cell the size of this square could run a torch bulb forever. Do you want to run a torch bulb forever Eugene?"

He didn't let Eugene answer that question either. He drew a second square. The two squares he explains would power fractionally more than two torch bulbs, because the first square has already crossed the threshold of insignificant power, thus from now on we can be sure the equation will be linear. Four squares are one square to the power of two.

"I love mathematics. I love," he pauses, "Its elegant."

Eugene Klein could tell that he did, just by the way that he says it, the sheer exuberance of the claim. Eugene, however neither loves nor understands words like, linear equations, and powers of two. He wishes Martin McKenzie would simply explain his wonderful idea, so he can return to his map. Eugene sits on the rim of the Museum dome, a vast glass and steel structure built into the roof. He stretches back raising his arms so that at full stretch he notices he can grab the two adjacent steel girders.

Martin has reached sixteen squares, he is sitting on the Museum roof with his piece of chalk, a steel square and a logarithmic table. He is no longer lighting torch bulbs with linear equations but heating or cooling entire galleries of the Victorian Museum. He knows, to a square inch, how large an area he would need to heat every winter by five degrees and cool every summer by seven, the entire four wings of the Victorian Museum.

"A single wing", Martin's explanation concludes, "I could cool by nine degrees, a single gallery by fifteen. If we extrapolate that downwards, into your workshop I could unleash a blizzard."

Eugene has wedged his left and right arms and left and right feet into two parallel girdles of the glass and steel dome and by extracting one limb at a time has managed to gully climb nine feet, or to the height of three glass panels up the face of the dome. When Martin mentioned blizzards, he released all four holds and slid with a crash to the ground.

A blizzard is exactly what Eugene desires.

Eugene apologizes for his ignorance of mathematic basics, but could Martin possibly, explain it again.

The second explanation is not concerned with numbers but the laying down of piping, a web of pipes for heating water by sunlight to ninety degrees celsius, the water then expands coils of cold ammonia, laid parallel to the water pipes, warming the ammonia, cooling the brine lines, in a three-way heat exchange, which in a nut shell, turns sunlight to ice.

"That," explains Martin, "Is my wonderful idea."

Eugene smiles.

Eugene Klein asks that Martin McKenzie, if he care to join him in his office for a chat. They'll need to put their heads down, thrash out the why's and wherefores of the blizzard they propose.

"We'll need." He hesitates, then spies upon Eugene's desk, the snow-jar of Lake Zakopane. He tilts it up, the snowflakes swirl, a blizzard raging through the trees.

"We'll need." He tilts it up again. "To build something like this, except, of course a larger size, big enough to walk inside. There we'll let your blizzards rage over hills and frozen lakes."

"The land my father wrote about, in which he saw the tiger-wolf."

They study Eugene's sketches; precise, cross-section drawing of the landscape envisaged, a contour map in millimetres of lakes and tiny ridges, boulders and escarpments of a landscape where wolves roamed.

There are problems of construction, they discussed them one by one.

A. How can the brine lines be insulated to prevent heat loss.

B. Could the landscape would attain the necessary temperature of.

"Minus three degrees celsius."

Martin has calculated to great precision the highest possible temperature his artificial snow can be sustained at, "But we must, we absolutely must have twenty square metres of the stuff." Any less it seems and the tendency of this artificial snow to insulate itself will not occur.

Put simply, it would melt.

Martin's solution, the brine lines would form the base of every ridge and bump in the landscape around which they would pack permasnow, and polystyrene rocks.

C. How can they create a partially frozen lake? For a pond of water, in the lowest ambient temperature attainable in the dome will not freeze.

Martin has done the sums, added the figures, calculated the losses and gains and there is no getting away from it, this lake will be a wet one, not a skate about one.

Martin's solution; "Fake the lake. We'll use sheet of glass, laid on a polystyrene lake, blended in with large plastic drums of water, the level of both the water and glass would be even and if a crust of the thinnest ice formed on the water, a crust of frost on the glass it would give a perfect impression of a partially frozen lake. I would like very much like to strive for authenticity."

"I think," agrees Paul, "that is our challenge."

D. What kind of flora would grow in their snow-jar?

Eugene had considered using fibreglass models of the various heath and fen scrubs, pencil-pine and beeches.

But, "Why, why, why? When we might, we could, no I'm sure we would, be able to find each plant we need and create a fen that's living."

To this end Joseph bequeathed an indispensable aid, at the very bottom of the glass cupboard, in minutest detail, a map not of mountains but of plants, one by one, every plant he found growing on an acre of ground, how it varies with seasons and year by year, labelled with numbers starting at one and finishing at three hundred and seventy-two.

"It's like painting by numbers, we just can't go wrong." says Eugene unfurling a large brownish sheet, full of delicate notations on the Museum floor.

"It gels so well with our submission."

They would call their joint submission, "Mystery, Myth and Monsters?" It would be complete for submission on the third Thursday of May.

7. Rosalind proposes a theorem.

The wolf's pace, to and fro, to and fro, before Rosalind standing beyond the wire, a delicate, effortless trot which can, Jacky Lambert "Friend of the Zoo", explains, "Cover quite remarkable distances."

Rosalind had only wanted to know where the wolves are. She'd simply asked, "can you show me the wolves." Rosalind did not necessarily want a guide, but since she has, she is glad it is someone like Jacky, not some old Granny.

Jacky is twentyish, spiky haired and ear-ringed twentyish, who speaks in the same rapid, intense manner as Rosalind. A little too much like Rosalind, thinks Rosalind who also thinks she might be being mimicked. She has nine tenths of a Master's degree. "In quokkas not wolves," she admits, "but try me I might know the answer."

She has, after all, seen them once, she tells Rosalind as they walk along the Zoo central avenue, flanked by the monkeys on the left and the merry-go-round on the right towards the far northern fence and the wolf enclosure. "I watched a pack of eight crossing Alaskan hills from a Piper Cherokee aeroplane. I saw at first just one grey moving spot, then another and another. I counted eight wolves crossing, long gullies of snow, outcrops of rock, gullies of snow. Although it was neither the closest nor the longest of sightings, it is a magical thing to watch living creatures on this earth."

She smiled, and her smile was both quicker and more spirited, than Rosalind had imagined.

"It was then that I realized that it is not the wolves of our childhood which are frightening, but that there may soon exist a world in which wolves do not roam. That is why I am to be a zoologist, why I have joined the Friends of the Zoo. Although it is not the zoo I am friends with rather the inmates, a necessary evil, an ark, if you will, for the battle will be about country; without their country a wolf is no more, and all the science in the world cannot stop that. So Rosalind, I ask you, what is foremost for you, the wolf or the science about it. The wolf doesn't, know, doesn't need, doesn't care about theorems or numbers. The science is our stuff the wolf doesn't care, the wolf only cares about country."

Rosalind Son-Lee didn't agree, the girl is obviously wacky, not a good source but the one which she has, it's time to ask her some questions.

To ask;

"What kind of animal is a wolf?"

"In what kind of landscape would you find it?"

A northern landscape, is the obvious answer, but what, Rosalind asks, makes a landscape suitable for wolves? This Rosalind thought was the key or a clue, and for this Rosalind invented a theorem.

Rosalind's theorem, {in her own words} is that an identical environment will sometimes become precursor to identical solutions to exploit it. What she means is that if the Great Western Tiers can be shown to support a wolf population, then the wolf population, may indeed exist.

She does not explain this to Jacky. The wolf, after all, is her find.

She simply asks a series of questions to Jacky and poses a few private queries to herself.

She asks Jacky.

"Would the wolf prey on the small wallabies, the bush tailed possums, or would they be more likely to attack small prey, the Marsupial rats and antechinus, or anything and everything they could find?"

Jacky, like Rosalind, thought the last.

And would, "a wolf range over the entire area {naturally Rosalind did not refer to what area she is referring to} or confine themselves to the woodlands and alpine margins?"

They both thought the range would be extensive, although perhaps seasonal.

"Would the wolf hibernate?"

"Perhaps."

"Would it run in a pack?"

"Not necessarily."

"Would its courtship be complex?"

"Probably."

"Would it mate for a lifetime or simply a season?"

They laugh.

To herself she poses the more disturbing questions.

"What if Joseph had accidently seen a mated pair amongst the conifers?"

"What if in the years when his find has entered into our mythology as a fraud the animal *Thylacine alpina* has vanished from our world?"

"Would we ever know? Could we ever prove it?"

And if it has not. If all the data confirms what she suspects already in her heart, that the wolf indeed did, does exist.

How could we save it? What should we do?

To this final question Rosalind Son-Lee has no answer.

8. Matinee.

Rosalind Son-Lee squats in her M.L.C. school uniform on the floor of Nat's cartoon room. She watches the Green Avenger descend through sixteen frames onto the picture postcard where her mother once stood. She watches the heroine Nadia dressed in black leather flying jacket emerges through the trees, to confront the passive face of the hero with the beautiful face of the heroine. She watches, Nadia, appropriately spirited and resourceful, bundle up the parachute and wisp it away while explaining to the "Avenger" succinctly and quickly, the situation, viz-a-viz entering the Reich land over the pass.

"We need to be careful and we need to be quick."

Nadia whispers "hurry" in Gothic print many times as she, the Green Avenger and their guide, an Italian mechanic from Bolzano climb precarious goat tracks zigzagging towards the pass. They leave the cover of conifers entering low alpine heath, and from heath to rock and lichen exactly as it ought to be on this textbook alpine pass, which Nat has copied, from a National Geographic, "Atlas of the world". Rosalind can recognize the copse of conifers, the two peaks which form the col, the neat layers of forest heath rock. The cartoon cuts to a map of Europe on which Nat illustrates, where the action takes place and where the war rages all around them. The only evidence of war in Nat's cinematography are the partisan's rifle and the tension measured by the tempo of Nadia's "hurry". There are many frames of ice-axe blades chipping monotonously upwards, many frames of a long tumbling fall below. Neither of which are what the schoolgirl Rosalind wants to see.

What Rosalind wants to see is that moment on the pass between Austria and Italy, when the mechanic from Bolzano has retreated the ice-steps down, and a hero eyes his lady, the way they do in movies, with that kind of twinkle that makes you know it's going to be sad, and happy and sad.

Rosalind wants Nat's movie to have those moments in it, but she cannot tell him that, in case he misunderstands, in case he thinks she is thinking about him and her or her and him, and anyway he should know that a movie is a movie and they are too young for anything seriously, serious. That's what Rosalind told her mother and her father and herself. Her mother laughed. What if Nat laughed, that would be horrid. He will not laugh because she will not tell him.

As Nat's cardboard reel runs out of wax-paper and the white torchlight shines how it shines at the end, Rosalind tells Nat.

"Colin Bradshaw made a film, in nineteen twenty eight he made a film with your great grandfather, on the tiers, it's in the journals in German." She shows him the account translating freely from the German of his Great Grand-father's amusement with this comic invention.

Nat turns off the projector. He doesn't turn on the light and he doesn't say anything for such a long span of seconds that Rosalind begins to believe she'd said absolutely the wrong thing. Then he says very softly in the manner she imagined of his heroines "hurry."

"It would be fun I think to find that."

It would be more than fun, it may be a clue. it may be the biggest clue of all, for what if he had filmed the wolf?

Nat explains there are many places such a film could be and many places it certainly isn't. It isn't in the study, for his uncle has removed everything from every cupboard, every draw and every box in the study and spread it in piles across the floor. It isn't in the office, for they both have searched through the office. It isn't in Nat's cartoon room, and it isn't in the empty gallery six where Eugene and Martin McKenzie are measuring floor space for a relief map of the Tiers.

The film, if it still exists, is certainly in the Museum, part of the "Klein Bequest", and it is certainly somewhere in the South West Wing.

Nat has made many expeditions into the storerooms of the south west wing. There are many storerooms all of which are cluttered with decades of accumulated junk. Official attempts to either clean-up or file what have accumulated have all met with failure. The one unofficial attempt to map the contents of the south west wing storerooms was begun two years ago by Nat Klein, who therefore considers himself the lone authority on the storerooms.

To find anything in the storerooms you need expertise. Nat's expertise. And a plan, Nat's plan. Nat's plan is invention number twenty-seven A. in his very private book of inventions and like every other invention expect the projector, it hasn't worked yet.

On Saturday in the room where he found the Korean Tripitaka and the room where he found the Shanghai telescope. They will try it.

9. Invention 27.

In the room where Nat found the jaguar claw, Rosalind and Nat sit cross legged on the floor eating Chinese take-aways from a restaurant on Celestial Avenue. They eat from plastic bowls and Ming Dynasty jade chopsticks, a matching set since both are green, according to Nat. As they eat Rosalind demands an explanation, a plan, a method by which Nat believes they can find anything, anything at all, amongst all this clutter.

Nat produces a sheet of paper on which he draws two lines at ninety degrees to each other. The first line is the height of the room, on the bottom of this line he writes the year nineteen twelve, the date he believes the room was first used as a storeroom and on the top the year nineteen thirty-seven, the date the room was filled to the rafters. The horizontal line is naturally the floor. Nat quickly draws the shelves and boxes which clutter the storage room until he has reached the highest stack of boxes on top of boxes, on top of boxes, jammed beneath the ceiling beams. In his notation this is the level called R.A.15, {Rafter Altitude No.15.}

He tells Rosalind once, he tells her twice, that this is the only known explanation to the storerooms, but Rosalind still asked if there is anyone at all, for there must be someone who could look the film up in the catalogue under "F".

The second part of his plan is the difficult part. It has to do with his invention number twenty-seven A, "the flying scaffold." Invented for this very reason to gain access to the high nooks and crannies of the storeroom.

Invention twenty-seven is a number of extendible wicker crevasse ladders belonging to the Ross Glacier Expedition of nineteen twenty eight. It is six ladders, all of which he proposes to hang from the ceiling by no4 nylon climbing slings and climbers steel clips, karabiners, Nat correctly calls them. To form a rough wicker scaffolding, an inclined ladder leading to a horizontal ladder, leading to an inclined ladder, in the manner of a fire escape, from the floor level to a high point just below the ceiling, onto these Nat proposes they climb.

"Of course, you are joking, you are joking Nat?"

Since he climbs up one, she guesses he's not.

Nat climbs onto the first wicker ladder and from that vantage point secures the second, the third and the forth, ascending towards the objective of the high boxes beneath the rafters.

Here he sits his head tucked under the ceiling pulling boxes out of the stacks and onto the wicker wings of his "flying scaffold." Boxes full of so many things wrapped in newspaper, The Argus, November nineteen thirty-six, the Age nineteen thirty-three.

He waves down to Rosalind, it's time she came up.

Rosalind ascends confidently the first vertical ladder, nervously shimmers along the first horizontal. It sways, she thinks, menacingly. She holds her breath and whispers.

"Just a little longer, just a little further", she refrains from whispering, "I know I can, I know I can." which would be juvenile.

Edging forward she wishes to appear more than anything else not as fearful as she feels. She doesn't look down, she looks along at Nat who stretches a hand to meet her, a surprisingly delicate hand, delicately caught amongst the ropes and ladders, and he does not let go of her hand immediately and she does not wish him to.

She tells him, as calmly, as measured of breath as she can, that in the journals there are many lists, although none which are final of, the "Klein Bequest" an average of these lists would take up a large sea-chest. She does not expect to find a sea-chest, it is only, she says, a concept.

All through that cool rainy May afternoon in the south west wing Rosalind learns a little and a little more about Nat's invention twenty-seven. It is she discovered a unique scaffolding, for it can rise and fall via a two-pulley system lowered and raised in tandem. On it a person can fly up and down, checking the stacks out for things to be found. Travelling backwards and forwards in time from Katmandu to Krakow, Kangaroo to Komodo. She learns much about the storeroom but found not the slightest clue.

10. Rosalind Son-Lee finds it!

Rosalind spent that long rainy afternoon gaining the confidence she will need to return on Sunday morning to fly the ladders solo over the stacks, to find between Kangaroo paws and Korea one large box of papers labelled the "Klein Bequest".

This is it.

She is sure this is it.

Somewhere in this pile of papers she'll find more than a clue, more than a note scribbled in the margin. She'll find the proof itself.

The first papers aren't promising, a mere, rehash of all she has read before. "In nineteen twenty three," she begins, "accompanied by Colin Bradshaw, photographer, Arlo Levi, medic, I began an expedition into the central plateaux of Tasmania. The objective of this expedition being twofold, to chart the extensive lake system and to profile its recourses."

What follows is yet another version of the first and subsequent expeditions differing little in substance but slightly in detail from the journals.

There are photographs of the party standing outside lake Sidon camp, Joseph splendid in Cossack hat and fur coat, Colin Bradshaw in English mountaineer breeches and anorak. There is a collection of five photographs which together complete a one-hundred-and-eighty-degree view from the summit of the Temple. Photographs of the bush tailed possums, Tasmanian devils, and Dusky antechinus, enough meteorological data to confirm the expected Sub-alpine climate, intricate descriptions of plant communities, patterns of snow and rain, volumes of water collecting on and flowing from the entire realm of the tiers.

Rosalind telephones Nat from the pay phone in the foyer.

He sounds gruff, he sounds like her father sounds when she has done something particularly silly, except Nat isn't as convincing.

He says, "The ladders are dangerous."

Yesterday, while he was coaxing her onto his famous "flying scaffold" they were as safe as houses.

He says, "You shouldn't be in the "Staff Only" sections."

When he always asks her to meet him there.

He says, "I'm very busy."

"To busy," she asks him, "to come and see what she has found?"

"Perhaps", he answers.

And Rosalind begins to believe she must have imagined yesterday he held her hand so gently. To believe, Elizabeth's right about boys being annoying, of course she would know. Boy, would she know.

Nat couldn't remember when they'd agreed that Rosalind ought to be the leader of this exploration. How it had come that Rosalind could enter his Museum, whenever she liked. She hadn't asked him to meet her this morning, he's sure she hadn't. Maybe, just maybe Rosalind just assumed he'd be there, and when he gets there she'll smile very blithely and shrug her shoulders as though it were Nat's fault. Maybe, but not likely because Nat is furious.

All the way into the city on the number twenty-three tram, he wonders and wonders what it takes to understand this girl, who is probably his girlfriend.

The girl who scampers up the first vertical ladder, fuming. Dances across the first horizontal ladder, annoyed. Leap-frogs up the first angled ladder, feeling slightly put out. And jitterbugs along the long vertical extension feeling a glimmer of pride in herself and so she ought, she bloody well ought, for as she yells, "Rosalind Son-Lee has found it". On Swan Street Nat Klein begins with the simplest of reasons why Rosalind should have stayed off the scaffold. The first and simplest reason is because she is a girl. The second is almost as simple minded as the first, because it is mine. The third because he had wanted them to find it together is also the least true, though he thinks he should stick with the third one.

Nat rehearses, his, I'm very annoyed speech from Swan Street to Swanson Street, from the fire escape door to the room where he found the jaguar claw and up till the moment he sees Rosalind on the highest of ladders waving him ecstatically up. At that moment he forgets all his silly reasons and just wants to know what she'd found.

She shows him the papers, the reports, the maps, all of which he flicks through quickly looking for the film.

"There has to be more."

"Yes," she nods, "there must be."

He tells her then, they can adjust the scaffold, to give it more flexibility, "the scaffold can fly," another relay here, another relay there, it's all very simple and all very safe and when he has finished, it will be Rosalind's role to test pilot the latest addition. Afterall you're the lightest, and I'm stronger than you.

He shows her how the second pulley systems can alter the position on the back wall, and therefore the position of the wicker ladder. How he can control both from a position on the floor.

She will need to wear the flying cap and goggles, an oversized leather jacket. She will need to buckle herself into a wicker pilot's seat of Nat's construction. From the north east corner, they will run the flying ladder towards the south wall. Very gently Nat begins pulling both belays simultaneously. The ladder and Rosalind are very much harder to move than he had expected but ever so slowly they begin their journey across the ceiling. The ladder moves steadily changing direction as Nat pulls on the second pulley. Rosalind stern faced behind the pilot's goggles glides over his control position towards the southern wall.

Nat yells, "Wow". This is how he'd always dreamt it would look like, gliding so smoothly, so beautifully, so flightfully.

He says, "Wow" again.

Rosalind says, "Wow" because it is so beautiful to fly, because Nat's invention has worked, and she is amazed.

Just as Rosalind says, "Wow", it broke.

The steel pin holding the south east pulley system broke. It wasn't Nat's fault. It really wasn't, but that didn't stop Rosalind descending unplanned into the boxes and boxes stacked on the ceiling of the storeroom.

There is a very loud crash as Rosalind Son-Lee riding the ladder disappears into the debris.

Nat says, "Damn" and decides almost then and there to rescue his girlfriend before he works any further on the design.

He jams another wicker ladder up against a stack of tea chests and climbs nearly to where Rosalind's landed. It leaves a metre and a half scramble over precarious boxes and then the undisciplined stacks above storeroom to find the rope which leads to Rosalind lying face down in a broken tea-chest. Nat reaches under Rosalind's arms wraps an arm around her shoulders and begins to lift her upright.

"It broke Nat."

"It sure did."

Rosalind is resting on Nat's knees, his arms remaining wrapped around her have fallen now into her lap. She holds his arms but not his hands within her own. She leans back slightly resting her head into the crook of his shoulders. His lips touch her face.

Is this a kiss?

Is this what it is like? Nat asks Nat. But before he can answer, Rosalind stretches her hand to pick something fallen from the tea-chest, a small ceramic shape wrapped in rice paper.

"A paw print."

A large canine print, could it be, she whispers, it could only be, the wolf print.

For the next two hours Rosalind forgets completely, Nat has finally kissed her, what reminds her of Nat's moist lips is Jacky Lambert lifting a large tortoise shell magnifying glass to her eyes to examine the ceramic shapes she had unwrapped from the rice-paper. It is the same magnifying glass Jeremy had given Nat, the one he had used to invent projection.

She cannot tell Jacky that, about that being why she had to smile, and she cannot concern Jacky with her faint worry that Nat may not understand why she had to dash from the Museum with her find, that she wasn't running from him but only to confirm what she was so, so certain of then. That it is, it really is the paw print of the wolf. She couldn't let Jacky think she was thinking about Nat, when together they were intelligently discussing science.

Jacky asks Rosalind, what she though science should be? And then answers herself, the way conceited people are prone to do.

"At this moment science is a tortoise shell glass. And what do we see in the glass?" She asks raising it from the table and staring into the ceramic image of a footprint. "I see uncertainty, while you see a thylacine and who", she asked, "is the glass deceiving?"

11. A sub-committee seeks a decision.

The subcommittee in charge of exhibitions sits on the third Thursday of every month. They sit in the administration wing, on the third floor, in a stuffy room with an uninteresting view over Swanson Street, Melbourne. For many years now the subcommittee has requested, that there meeting room be moved into the ministerial offices, on the fourth floor, on the south side, looking over Treasury Gardens.

"A glorious view inspires glorious decisions." Or so they began their bi-annual request, in triplicate. The request is, and has been, for as many years, before the subcommittee in charge of office allocation.

Naturally this subcommittee has a splendid view, from which they watch with delight, couples promenading through the gardens. They are not of the opinion that, the more glorious the view, the more glorious the decision, and they should know. Meanwhile the five ministerial officers drive six city blocks to sit with the one Museum representative and view proposals.

They like models. "A model is worth a thousand words."

They hate words, pages and pages of gobbledygook they find mostly incomprehensible while models can simply be looked at, seem with just a glance. No one has suggested, though they might, that a good model is like a good view.

They considered Morgan Travis's model for the "Mist of Time" exhibition to be a classic. It wasn't, as they said, "Muddied up by science." It was very visual, and it brought out once again the ever-favourite dinosaur bones. "The kids love them." The kids, and this is the general Museum view, may not love an exhibition titled "Mystery, Myth, and Monsters," and the giant glass dome has as far as they can see, nothing inside it other than snow. Plain, fluffy, white stuff, not at all interesting, and most of the submission, is well muddy with science.

The subcommittee cannot decide. Many times, they have approached the subject and from many angles. They would like to decide. They would like there to be an answer, which everyone agrees upon, which everyone is happy with, which won't return one day to haunt their careers. What the subcommittee in charge of exhibitions is waiting for is a sign. A sign driving down Swanson Street on a tramcar number eight, a sign bearing the *Thylacine alpina* advertising beer. But this sign does not come, nor any other, only a rumour.

The rumour is "the zoo is interested in the Thylacine." Such a rumour cannot be ignored.

There exists a subcommittee in charge of Zoological exhibits, they meet in the Zoological gardens in a very pleasant room overlooking an artificial wetland. If any subcommittee confirms the adage, "a glorious view inspires glorious decisions," it is they. They have had some wonderful exhibits. The gorillas, the pandas, the snow leopard, they have upstaged Museum time and time again. The subcommittee in charge of Zoological exhibits are cunning. They could have invented the rumour. The rumour may have begun in their committee room.

Whatever the source of the rumour it cannot be ignored. What if the Zoo beat them to the Thylacine. That must not happen, whatever this Thylacine is, the zoo must not have one.

"After-all the dam things dead isn't it, and dead things belong to us."

"Here, here, they agreed."

And stamped their approval on Eugene Klein's proposal. Provisional approval, before they begin to re-draft a letter which asked, that the minister consider the savings of one taxi fare instead of the five currently used in the extravagant set-up due to poor allocation of space in the section. Why one simple move could save him a fortune. They'd be willing to hold meetings in a room with a view.

12. In Which Nat thinks of Rosalind and Rosalind the Wolf.

Under a black umbrella and wrapped in a bright red fibre-pile jacket in a limpid late May drizzle, the only possible source of the rumour stands waiting impatiently for Rosalind who is a quarter of an hour late, which is not like Rosalind. She looks at her watch, shakes water off her sleeves, and shivers slightly, watching the wolves pacing long, damp strides. She thinks of leaving in twenty minutes time, but notices as she thinks it, Rosalind come running. Rosalind waves brightly from the path running down beside the Asian Black bears. It is the wave she'd greeted Nat Klein with when she'd found the first boxes of the Klein Bequest. It is a wave of victory. She has new evidence, uncovered yesterday evening in what she calls, "the digs".

Jacky has not seen the digs, she has heard enough to imagine Nat's complex rigging of suspended ladders into the level they have christened, "Klein 2." From the digs came the footprints. The footprints were a poser. They are probably fake. Jacky would consider that probability a high eighty percent. Twenty percent of Jacky Lambert wonders, what if?

Rosalind has a series of photographs. Taken from the moving picture, they have finally found. The photographs are of poor quality. The film worse. Nat was bitterly disappointed. Faded ghosts on a faded background stood before the tents of ghosts, shaped like inverted ice-cream cones. Only the title is comprehensible, it is "The Ascent of Mount Jerusalem". The photographs are undoubtedly of a creature, a large wolf like creature. Rosalind considers it an argument that the photo is so unclear. "If it is a fraud, why produce a photograph so vague?"

"But that," resists Jacky, "Is not an argument. It is again a poser but not an argument that such a scientific man should fake so unconvincing a fraud."

"I have thought about it Rosalind, thought about it often, and what I cannot find is the answer to one question. Why would a man invent a wolf?"

A silly question in Rosalind's view. The same silly question which has tied up Eugene. Only Rosalind, in her view, can see this problem clearly, beyond the presence of Joseph Klein and his heroic expeditions. If the wolf exists, and she is not saying, yes or no, it exists solely because the wolf is, a biological necessity, that is all.

Nat lay in the bedroom dark, having read the last pages of John Buchan's Greenmantle, wondering if Jeremy is asleep yet. He whispers, "Jeremy". Jeremy doesn't answer. He whispers "Jeremy", again. Once again Jeremy doesn't answer, but this time Nat knows he is awake. He is lying too still and breathing too regularly, the way he does when he's pretending to sleep, when he's ignoring Nat. Nat flashes his torch into his brother's eyes. He is not, or no longer, asleep.

"What Nat?" he asks in his tired voice.

"If a mysterious girl kissed you would you kiss her back?"

That is the question which has been worrying Nat. Jeremy doesn't answer straight away. He never does. As Jeremy considers his answer, Nat flashes his torch across the ceiling of their bedroom. The torch is a searchlight. A searchlight which will strike the wing of the model Lancaster, hanging from the ceiling on five-millimetre fishing-line, a Messerschmitt 105 attacks the bomber at an angle almost directly in line with his pillow. A Halifax bomber and two spitfires form a second bombing party above Nat's desk. One by one the searchlight picks each up. "Ack, ack, ack," Nat whispers, and once again the legendary gunner Nat Klein saves his Great Uncle's Lancaster.

Jeremy asks, "Are we talking about Rosalind?"

Nat lowers the torch to his doona. "Maybe it's not anyone, maybe I'm only asking if it did happen like if it was in a script."

Jeremy folds his arms back behind his head. He is smiling. "Surely the Green Avenger is the type of hero who would find no woman mysterious."

Nat always has to explain how it is with the Avenger, growing up as he did in the Son Buddhist Monastery Songwang-sa. What did he learn there of woman and worldliness? Nothing at all. What did he learn there of the Buddhist mind? Nothing at all. For that is how it is with the Buddhists, forever using the same words for entirely different answers. Nat tries again to explain, that it is the nature of hero's that between them and the heroine alliances form, alliances of passion. Nadia is a patriot of passion; whose passion is liberty. The Green Avengers passion is righteousness, they are therefore only allies of the moment.

Rosalind Son-Lee's passion is not the Thylacine but science. Nat's passion is not the Thylacine but the world he can create on a matt white wall. Their's is not even an alliance of the moment, although this has not occurred to Nat.

It has however occurred to Rosalind.

PART 3.

A Snow Jar Named Desire

Melbourne Age December 1982
And so it begins;

About 170 conservationists and 150 police are gathered close to the tiny town of Strahan in what appears to be a showdown over the proposed Gordon below Franklin Dam. A spokesperson for the Wilderness Society said all the volunteer protestors had received one days training in non-violent ways to obstruct the dam contractors.

A spokesman for the H.E.C. asks simply that the protestors do not interfere with the legitimate construction of the Gordon below Franklin dam. A local Queenstown miner voiced the more forceful opinion that, "those bloody mainlanders should piss off and leave Tasmania for Taswegians"

13. Nat and Rosalind expand an idea.

The Tuesday evening Nat put pen to paper and drew the first black lines of the Seventh Samurai standing on a U-boat approaching Trieste harbour was the evening the hammering began in the gallery number five, South West Wing.

The giant dome had begun. It began as an enormous wooden frame ecliptic in shape and as high as the two storied gallery ceiling. It began by lying on the gallery floor as six semi-circular frames each larger than the next like two enormous butterfly wings. A butterfly which two days later raises both wings in a single elegant motion for the prefabricated frames had been hinged and lashed together in such a way that to drag on one pulley lifted the entire ensemble. Two magnificent wings rose and formed a snow-jar. On the inner and outer shell, they fixed clear plastic sheet then between the two at various junctures they pumped pressurized insulation foam.

On Wednesday evening Nat and Rosalind stood inside a near complete shell of Eugene Klein's snow-jar.

"It's so huge," Rosalind asks perplexed. "Why is it so huge? It doesn't need to be that big. What are they doing? Is this supposed to be science or a side show? What are they going to do with this enormous dome? And how do they monitor it?"

At least to the last question Nat has an answer.

"They monitor it from the room beside Eugene's office."

On a long bench Martin has screwn with papers, some of which comprise the program for the snow-jar, some of which are miscellaneous jottings on ideas in progress and some are cast off shopping lists. A large I.B.M. computer faces them. It is turned on.

Rosalind reads the first page of the program and says, "Tut."

She reads the second and says, "Oh no."

She reads the third, the forth, and the fifth before reaching the disheartening conclusion, that, "They are using one thousand K. of intellect as a thermo-stat."

"Do they know what they are doing?"

Nat shrugs.

Rosalind sits at the keyboard pursing her lips. She begins to twist her right hand around her left index finger, telling Nat, she just cannot believe it. And then she begins to tinker. As she begins to tinker, she explains to Nat, just what they should do with this intellect.

"They should build a program which duplicates in the dome all we have gleamed about the climate of the Great Western Tiers during the era of exploration. The daily temperatures, wind speeds, snow falls, rain and sleet. All the seasonal variances, of ice and snow cover, everything should be the same, and then we could ask the program many questions. Such as, what kind of carnivore could survive this? They could ask the program to project population numbers of any species and whether they are active? If the Thylacine is hungry what can it eat? If it is freezing where could it go? They could program a one degree drop in temperature and ask, what species are no longer viable? A one degree rise in temperature and ask, which are now viable? They could have done so many things, but they haven't, they haven't even got the temperatures right."

Rosalind Son-Lee begins to do what they said that they ought, she lowers the temperatures ten degrees celsius and doubles the wind speed. She begins to enter each known animal into the program with a description of food source, shelter and courtship, and everything known about possible prey. Asking Nat if he could draw a likeness of each.

"That's great." smiles Rosalind, "what a cute antechinus and what a brute of a wolf."

Day by day they keep adding and snipping and changing.

"Do you think it is possible to put in the film."

"And what of the paw prints, your wonderful theorem about those precursors and solutions and wolves."

Until they arrive at a program which Martin and Eugene ought to find such an improvement on the one that they had drawn.

"It's lucky that we're here," Rosalind says proudly.

"I'm glad that we did it." Nat Klein agrees.

All the while Nat assisted, re-programming of the snow-jar, he had thought, what a shame, there is no way to see, all the fine drawings he has made of these creatures, all his drawings of lake banks and mountains and mist. He tried to think of a way, both simple and subtle, that people might see them, at least he and Rosalind, and Martin and Eugene.

It was on Thursday that he thought of the answer, such a simple solution he should have thought it before. What he needs is just waiting for someone to retrieve it from down in the basement in a storeroom marked "T". It is not simply one but twelve televisions which he stacks one upon the other, like the N.A.S.A. space centre room.

"But this", he tells Rosalind, "is only the beginning, for his plan to succeed he will also need cameras, but cameras are not yet relics to be found amongst debris, deep in basements of the south western wing. Cameras must be borrowed, albeit unofficially from the Audio-Visual Department, two wings away.

14. Burglary.

Rosalind didn't realize, when they started this program, that it would lead to relocating, from one wing to the other, things which aren't necessarily theirs to remove.

"Why don't we just ask?" Rosalind kept saying.

"Who could we ask? Who around here would listen, to two people, they think are merely just kids?"

Rosalind concedes, he is right, about asking, but why, she's complaining do we have to use black shoe polish all over our faces and over our hands.

"After all Nat, I'm quite dark already."

The black polo-neck skivvy, the black jeans and balaclava, she thought them becoming in a rat-baggy way.

"You look grand." says Nat to the burglar Rosalind and she had to agree.

"I do, don't I Nat."

He explains his new plan, it is quite simple, no slings or karabiners, no ladders or ropes, just a, "stand on my shoulders and into the window, no trouble at all."

Rosalind being the lightest will be the one shoulders. Nat being the strongest will be on the ground. It may be easy for Nat but Rosalind's left wondering if another of Nat Klein's plans won't end like the rest with Rosalind landing with a thump on her bum.

"Are you ready Rosalind, it's time we began."

To tip-toe so quietly along deserted, dark corridors, Nat with the flash-light flicking forward and back, stalking through Mammalia, tiger's eyes beaming, between the slivering pythons flanking Reptilicias door, they pass boa-constrictors, anacondas and taipans, crocodiles waiting jaws permanently open, their white teeth flashing in Nat's beam of light. All through Progress their thieving hearts clanging, up via the stair-well to sneak their way in, to the Staff Only section, where the grave danger lies, of detection, apprehension, maybe arrest.

They follow the plan and a map of Nat's, a map with small footprints drawn along corridors, through appropriate galleries and up the stairs-wells. A plan to bunk Rosalind up to a window usually left open above the locked door. The map has one problem, one miscalculation, the problem is simple, the windows too high.

Nat is five feet six, Rosalind five feet one, elementary mathematics is enough to prove she must stand on Nat's shoulders before her centre of gravity can pivot through the window, the same mathematics would also have proved that Rosalind pivoting through the window, cannot reach the lock of the door beneath her, cannot go forwards and cannot go back. Only when Rosalind is stuck, her feet in the corridor, her torso in the Audio-Visual room does Nat consider this problem he euphemistically describes as, "Rosalind's descent."

"On my head," whispers Rosalind a little too loudly.

"Think laterally," he suggests, realizing the solution would have been a crevasse ladder or two and perhaps some ropes, slings, or maybe but he wouldn't suggest this now, the cameras were not the best idea he has ever had.

He suggests a ladder at least to return her back to the safety of the corridor.

"You're not leaving me Nat?"

"No," he says, he wouldn't.

And while he sits on the corridor floor thinking of the things he could do and the things he may well have done better, he watches her legs kick and they look rather funny. He watches them squirm, re-aligning themselves horizontal rather than perpendicular to the wall, and disappear.

He expects a plop as he watches her legs disappear and is quite surprised to hear nothing at all until some minutes later when Rosalind steps out with the cameras.

"This is the last time Nat Klein, the very last time."

Rosalind doesn't stay angry for as long as Nat expected. As soon as she begins setting the cameras up in the snow-jar, plugging them into the television screens, she forgot for a while, why she is so angry, so justifiable furious with Nat tonight.

They turn on the cameras, turn on the sets, turn on the program and sit down to wait. Just for a moment, before everything works, pictures are coming from all over the place. Inside the snow jar and all that Nat's drawn is creeping and crawling all over the land. The land's not quite ready, the program needs work, work on the edges and work in the guts.

"But you can see where I'm going, you can see where I'm at."

Rosalind could see it, "It's beautiful Nat."

It took Eugene Klein three quarters of an hour to convince Martin McKenzie not to kill Nat.

He pointed out, that the television camera really was a great idea.

The television screens can be placed in the public viewing area, therefore solving a problem which had been nagging at them for some weeks, the problem of heat loss. The bigger the windows the more heat they would lose, and they couldn't afford to lose much heat, or the snow would all melt. It had never occurred to either Eugene or Martin, and now they wonder why, in all their designs, in all their calculations seeking a perfect compromise between the ability of the snow-jar to retain heat and the need for the viewing public to see the world within that, nobody needs ever actually look inside the snow-jar. They only need to believe, they are looking. And there is nothing people believe more, than what they see on T.V.

The world inside the snow jar had just expanded immeasurably.

15. Martin McKenzie turns on the Brine.

On the thirteenth of June on a clear blue winter Sunday Martin McKenzie turns on the brine and the temperature in the snow-jar plummets. It falls seventeen degrees celsius on the visual displays and snows for fourteen hours. It is frightening.

Martin McKenzie watches the monitors. Eugene Klein watches the monitors. Nat Klein and Rosalind Son-Lee watch the monitors, which display a continuous update of climatic data plus images from within the snow-jar.

Ambient Temperature	minus 5 degrees C.
Ground Temperature	minus 7 degrees C.
Wind direction	south.
Wind Speed	10 knots.
Wind Chill	minus 17 degrees C.
Visibility	nil.
Precipitation	
As Rain	Zero.
As snow	25 mm.
Water Temperature	0.5 degrees C.
Depth of Ice	Zero.
Percentage Ice Cover	Zero.

Updating, Ambient Temperature, minus seven degrees celsius, percentage ice cover, one percent. The monitors scan, a maelstrom unleashed in the confines of the snow-jar.

No one in the monitor room speaks.

No one in the monitor room had expected what they saw. Or didn't see for the mist spun in flurries beyond the cameras snowful and dizzy. The snow-jar rumbles like a Lancaster fuselage, exactly that terrifying rumble of war, though only Eugene recognizes that. Rosalind Son-Lee flicks vainly through her notebooks for her temperature parameters. Martin asks the

I.B.M. for updates on stress. And Nat looks into the land he has imagined so many, many times.

Here at last is a land built for heroes.

16. Eugene **Klein** has a Visitor.

Henk Van Der Sarr, Hydro Electricity Commission, Tasmania, Special Projects, the card read, enters Eugene's workshop unannounced and indignant, two weeks before the opening.

"I am disappointed Eugene."

He stands before Eugene in the monitor room, watching the television screen which display the climatic data, and live broadcasts of the world within. He flicks through Martin's loose notes. Picks up, scrutinizes and discards Eugene's many early designs. Reads aloud the text of the observation sheets Eugene Klein is proof reading.

The observation sheets will be provided to the tour parties, guided "through the ascent" as they euphemistically describe the thirty-nine steps into the dome. The observer sheets are Nat's idea, the text which Henk Van Der Sarr reads is also Nat's.

"It is nineteen hundred twenty three, the sun is about to set on the era of adventure, only a few corners of the world are left unexplored. One last unknown territory lies a day's climb from this camp. A mountain wilderness where on September the seventeenth nineteen thirty three an animal was sighted, a wolf, *Thylacine a lpina*: height, one hundred centimetres; weight, thirty kilograms; colour, light fawn to cream with darker stripes across its rump. Before us, a time capsule, stands waiting for us to enter."

The observer's sheets, are the size of a small notebook, printed in friendly olive green on fawn paper. Henk Van Der Sarr folds the observer's sheets into a fine pointed arrow which he uses to point out details on one of the many maps.

"The Bronte Park catchment, five thousand square kilometres, twenty-six thousand lakes, twelve rivers feeding a single generator of forty thousand kilowatts, there is beauty in electricity Eugene, your father foretold that in nineteen twenty four."

Henk Van Der Sarr cannot pronounce the letter F. This does not cause Eugene to feel any warmth towards Henk Van Der Sarr, who is not a warmth generating man. He is neither a tall man nor a particularly imposing man, except for the intensity of his gaze. A gaze which at that moment accesses Eugene, in light naturally of his father, an assessment Eugene loathes for its inequity.

"Do I see the toy?" He underlines the word toy with the faintest smile, it pleases him.

Eugene replies, "If you like." It would have been pointless to say no, Henk Van Der Sarr had only asked him out of impoliteness.

As they walk the corridor, Henk Van Der Sarr places the facts before Eugene. Facts, says Henk van Der Sarr, are the business of science.

"Fact one, your father believed in progress, dams, Eugene, dams are progress."

He looked Eugene coldly in the eye and continued.

"Fact two, your father spent sixty seven percent of his time researching hydrography, twenty six percent of his time researching botany and seven percent researching Zoology, of that seven percent he spent fifty five percent describing reptilicia, thirty three percent on the lower mammals and two percent looking for the wolf. What is two percent of seven percent Gene? Don't mind if I call you Gene, do you?"

In fact, he did mind.

"Fact three, the wolf is a fraud."

He pointed this out with a finger thrust into Eugene's rib-cage.

"Fact four, resurrecting the wolf will only darken your family name."

"Fact five, the wolf whatever its status is a Tasmanian wolf, and the Tiers whatever their status are the Tasmanian Tiers, and the status of anything on our island is what we wish it."

He did not elaborate whether us meant the Hydro Electricity Commission or his fellow Tasmanians.

Fact six, and this is a doozy, "Your father worked for us, you didn't know that, I find it is better to have all the facts."

It is minus two degrees celsius on the Tiers the Hydro doesn't control and snowing lightly. The monitors, a second set of which they have set up on the observation deck of the snow-jar, are scanning regularly through a three-hundred-and-sixty-degree arc, a landscape of low ridges and semi frozen lakes, scarce vegetation protruding above banks of snow a wispy southerly blowing five knots and rising. Henk Van Der Sarr looks through a selection of windows all of which are probably false, they are holographs rather than windows, neither Martin nor Nat could resist this final piece of trickery.

"Clever Eugene, so very clever, but where," he whispers with a venom, "where is your Thylacine?"

17. Rosalind and Nat spy an Opening.

Where indeed is the thylacine?

Rosalind Son-Lee would love to know.

Rosalind Son-Lee sits in Nat's pilot seat fidgeting with his leather hat and goggles on the day of the first official tour.

She is annoyed.

She is nervous.

She is pissed-off.

It would be, so terribly unfair, it would be, so terribly, terribly unfair, if someone in this party were the first to see the Thylacine.

The party is setting out in half an hour guided in the ascent by Martin McKenzie, dressed in 'Dry-as-a-bone' and slouch brimmed stockman's hat. A party of dignitaries, which does not include Rosalind and it does not include Nat. Rosalind is indignant.

"After all we have done" she stammered,

"If it wasn't for us," she fumed.

Yes, Nat nods, that is just how it is when you are not quite an adult and not quite a kid.

"I'd like to know, I mean I'd like to see. I guess I'd like to be, that spy on the wall when the tour enters our Observation Hide."

Rosalind sits on the work-bench, her feet hooked under Nat, who spins the swivel chair to the limit of his movement, clockwise, anti-clockwise, clockwise and back. He squeezes Rosalind's legs, runs his fingers up to her knee. Her knee is as high as he dares go, for Rosalind might slap him, as Elizabeth said so. Nat sits thinking of espionage and girls, not in that order.

Trying to imagine a way, sufficiently cunning and appropriately safe, to spy upon the opening tour.

There must be a way, there just must be a way, if only, if only he could think it.

And think it he did.

Think it he beams.

The most delicious thinking he's had in his life. He takes Rosalind's hand. He lifts Rosalind up, out of the pilot's seat and guides her to where the monitors are scanning a snow crusted day.

Nat keys in cameras five, six and seven, monitor one and sixteen, adjusts the angle of camera six one eighty degrees, the camera swings around, its view swings around with it, back through the windows into the Hide. For, "We bugged the snow-jar the day it was made."

Rosalind kisses him twice on the back of the neck and licks his ear as Elizabeth had told her, but it doesn't feel really grown up like French kissing does. Elizabeth will always tell her, when and what to do next, so she isn't too hasty, so she doesn't lose her self-respect. There are lots of things you can do before you cross that pale, some of them Rosalind cannot believe.

What pale have they crossed she wonders so guiltily to spy, Sir Benjamin Harris, Sir Randwick Clover sipping Great Western Sparkling Shiraz, discussing power and the application of solar coolers. They stand in Base Camp, Mersey River, a series of static displays in appropriate era tents before the snow jar entrance, Joseph Klekin's eyeglasses, Joseph Klein's sextant, which he did not process in nineteen twenty three, but not the gramophone which he did. Camp beds stiffly tucked, a camp basin below a camp mirror and camp shaving utensils. One stuffed wallaby (*Thylugale billardierri*) a brush tailed possum (*Tichusurus velpecula*), and a Tasmanian wild cat (*Dasgurus viver-innu*) all borrowed from Mammalia, and from Reptilicia the skinks (*Leilo-pisma ocellation* & *greeni*). And standing in the forecourt, sealed in a perplex case, a fibreglass replica of the *Thylacine alpine*.

"Is it very likely," Sir Richard asks, "That such an idea could run?"

Run is his word for that month, it is dynamic and that according to his deck calendar is the way life is meant to be lived.

"The question," he says, "of energy is the question of the future."

He'd met a man a week ago who'd told him that, an impressive man named, Henk Van Der Sarr. Energy is his business, energy and power, and not for the first time Sir Richard ponders the ambiguity of those words.

They spy, Bill Johnson mussing over the possibility of skiing length to breath of Martin's Tiers, to Anita Graige who simply scoffs.

"If Martin had wanted it skied he would have installed a poma".

Anita Graige brushes beautiful blonde hair with three fingers back, so blasé, but oh, so self-assured. Anita Graige spends two weeks of every year at Falls Creek, the best two weeks naturally, she deserves nothing less. Bill fumbles with the monitors while Anita turns her attention away, and Rosalind punches Nat in the midriff for staring.

She swivels the cameras in the direction of Martin laughing with Liam O'Rourke, who has never, seen so much ice out of a whisky glass.

"The men are more comfortable with the monitors, the women with the windows."

Rosalind has been ticking them off into two separate boxes. She has scribbled on her note-pad. One box for men, one box for women, ticks for the windows, crosses for the monitors. She is right. She begins to draw a new set of squares on a sheet of Eugene's graph paper. She commences to subgroup; women over fifty, men over fifty, men over fifty who wear corduroy jackets, women over fifty who wear silk head-scarfs, women over fifty who don't. She really is amazing is Miss Rosalind Son-Lee, who else would have thought to do something like that.

In the Observation Hide polite conversation prevails, the Tiers becomes a backdrop before which career journeys are mapped. Morgan Travis jokes familiarly with Sir Benjamin Harris while Martin eavesdrops. Morgan comments when prompted, for he doesn't, as he admits, covert the role of the critic, "being essentially a creator", but Martin and Eugene, you must admit have gone somewhat overboard on snow.

Seventy percent mist covers the ground, intermittent snow falls in the snow-jar. For almost an hour between one fifteen and two ten it has been clear and cold, visibility half way up the Mount Jerusalem escarpment, no-one could ask for more. It has clouded over as the opening progressed, and while it is snowing lightly, the visibility is still good. Eugene Klein pointedly explains, no more can they control the weather on Latrobe Street, than they can the weather in the snow-jar. Eugene describes this as an exercise in authenticity. Morgan Travis coined the phrase, "Eco-realism."

According to Rosalind Son-Lee's sheets Morgan Travis spent exactly seventy-two seconds watching the monitors, eleven seconds glancing through windows six and four, and three minutes twenty-five seconds staring at Anita Graige. It is not the least amount of time of any viewer, spent looking through the windows, it is the second least. Nor is it the most amount of time looking at Anita Graige, that was Bill Johnson. The least amount of time spent looking through the windows was one point five seconds by the girl in the polka-dot jump-suit while Nat for one and a half minutes had his eyes fixed solely upon her. Her name is Kathline Turner and she works in the library.

The day Nat met her was the day he decided, some-people look heaps better on T.V.

18. The Woman in the fez.

In the first fortnight beyond the opening Rosalind's observations begin to yield results, some more or less expected, one totally unexpected.

The results they might have expected are:

Ninety percent of the public less than thirty years old prefers to sit at the television consuls;

Sixty percent between thirty and sixty prefer the map displays and the least deceptive windows,

Ninety nine percent of sixty years plus prefer the static displays.

"Kids prefer the deceptive windows,"

Nat writes on the graph paper sheet, a purely subjective observation.

Rosalind drew no conclusions.

The unexpected result is: a woman wearing a fez, spent four point five minutes reading the printed information, two minutes looking at the maps and twelve minutes watching the consuls. She gave no indication she saw the thylacine, but in fact, she did, briefly, through a thin lake-side mist.

She only glances at the windows on the way out.

She came again one week later while Eugene Klein monitors the Observation Hide. It had first annoyed, then amused Martin and Eugene that Nat had spied on the public. Or more correctly it had mostly annoyed Martin and mostly amused Eugene, but that was before Martin saw the statistics. The statistics convinced Martin to establish a roster.

During Eugene's roster the woman in the fez returns. She is unusually dressed, in a Moroccan Fez, loose fitting Indian silk pants, a Thai hill tribe jacket. She is an unusually handsome woman of a certain age. She looks like the kind of woman who might have once said, her soul is an express train. She looks like the sort of woman it would be hazardous for Eugene to know.

She is wearing a T-shirt on which is printed the words, "The Society of the Wolf".

When Eugene notices the T-shirt, he knows it is a message. A message for him, he sprints from the workshop, along the corridor, down the fire escape to enter the south west wing via the back of the snow-jar. It is a silly way to go, they haven't made provision for entering the snow-jar that way, he must dash down the stairs into the basement and up the other side, by the time he has, she is gone.

She isn't in Reptilicia. She isn't in The Mechanical age. She isn't in Regalia, where Eugene quaintly expects to find her.

She is in the kiosk, buying a Ned Kelly postcard to send to her daughter Zoey in Helsinki, Finland.

"You don't mind," he asks, "If I interview your T-shirt."

The interview, Eugene conducts as a tour, a tour of many things as tours are want to be, which begins on the roof beside the solar coolers, and it begins with his answering her questions, rather than her answering his. Questions about his father, how he came to find the Thylacine? About himself, how he came to found the exhibit?

About the T-shirt and the Society, there is only one simple fact, there isn't one.

"I just invented it."

"Will you make another T-shirt?"

"Do you want to buy one?"

"No, I just want to know if anyone else does."

She smiles, the smile Eugene expects, the unnerving smile of a sparkler.

Mary O'Becket knows she is more than a T-shirt, more than a gag on a joke, however much she is also both. She is the mother of Zoey in Helsinki, Zoey who has inherited her wanderlust. And many things besides; Mary O'Becket has loved, has lost, has found and has given away. She once drove a Porsche, but now rides a push-bike, because freedom is worth it. And anyway, she didn't like that version of herself as much as she likes this one, who is lighter but has more substance.

Mary O'Becket, considers Eugene, as much as he does her. He is older than her and she prefers younger although younger is harder, much harder than it was a decade ago. He is handsome, was once very handsome, you can see it in his poise, in the ease of his talk, he is not afraid of her. And then, there is sadness, a deep enduring sadness. Mary O'Becket will not, no never, put her journey to Helsinki on hold for this or any other man, no never again, however intriguing he seems.

He is intriguing.

By July the sixteenth, seven sightings of the *Thylacine alpina* have been recorded on the observation sheets. Four cluster in the afternoon of July fourteen, three are random. They may or may not be authentic.

Rosalind is dismissive of the random sightings but interested in the cluster. The first recording is at two-fifteen, the second at two forty-seven and the third and fourth simultaneously at four thirty-five, on a clear but pungently cold day, frost lingering into the afternoon under high cirrocumulus cloud, wind speed one knot, wind direction west by north west.

On the day prior and the morning of the fourteenth, two tiny antechinus were sighted seventeen times, fifty percent above average, after the thylacine sighting the antechinus was sighted no longer, which poses two questions. How could the *Thylacine alpina* know that the game was there? What can this tell Rosalind about her Thylacine? Scent? Chance? Chance is too vagrant from a survival point of view, and scent assumes a very powerful nose. Rosalind prefers to think it was scent but has no proof.

And proof, as Jacky Lambert always says, is the business of science.

19. The Facts.

"Proof", as Henk Van Der Sarr said, "Is in the pudding."

Henk Van Der Sarr sets out a series of infra-red satellite photographs onto the table overlooking the artificial wet lands in the room where the Sub-committee in charge of exhibitions {Zoological} meet. The photographs are classified. He is overstepping his responsibility even admitting they exist, let alone displaying them, at least that is what he emphasises to these fellow bureaucrats around the subcommittee table, all or whom would understand the delicacy of overstepping one's responsibility.

There are ten sets of photographs. They are taken at different moments and from different degrees of magnification. Every photograph is centred on a point forty-one degrees fifty-minute south by one hundred and forty-six degrees twenty minutes east. This point is not surprisingly a lake. A small one hundred and twenty-two square metre lake one thousand three hundred metres above sea level on a plateau banking away from Mount Jerusalem. The lake is a very lightly coloured pink, its water temperature five degrees celsius. The lake has no name, it is one of twenty thousand lakes on the Tiers, it has no specific importance.

Henk Van Der Sarr as is his practice points out the facts, the first being, "Were busy people." In fact, the Subcommittee for Exhibitions {Zoological} are not in the slightest bit busy, but if Henk Van Der Sarr wants to think they might be, they are happy to play along with the illusion.

The subsequent facts are; the Hydro Electricity Commission has a vision, a vision of co-operation, of mutual development of man and nature. The Hydro Electricity Commission, he is loath to admit is disappointed in the Museum. Their exhibit, "have you seen it?" emphasizes the mythology at the expense of the facts.

"I myself am a European, as was the explorer Joseph Klein, I also understand the romance of the wolf, but we gentlemen are scientists, our concern is the facts."

Henk Van Der Sarr points to the facts, they are barely visible facts, they are very small facts indeed, they are exactly one hundred and twenty centimetres tall and weigh forty-five kilograms. They are alive. He is not saying they are wolves, he is an engineer, not a biologist, therefore he will not comment, except to suggest.

"In the interests of science, the Hydro would assist any responsible party who might wish to exhibit these facts".

Assist can be translated as under-right. He did not translate, "exhibit".

22. The Worth of a Dash.

By the twenty fourth of July there are seven unconfirmed sightings of the *Thylacine a lpina* all of which have been added to a relief map on display in the foyer and to the giant multicoloured map in Eugene's office. Eugene has positioned each unconfirmed sighting against the banks of Lake Sidon in the faintest orange possible. The three confirmed sightings of "The Society of the Wolf T-shirts" Eugene has noted on a large sheet of graph paper. Eugene Klein though more of the sightings of the T-shirts, than the sightings of the Thylacine. He wonders why Mary hadn't told him of the sales. She had promised she would.

It doesn't occur to Eugene that she simply isn't ready.

She hasn't decided what to wear. She hasn't decided what guise; what aspects of herself she is willing to share and what regalia would accomplish her ends. And she hasn't decided what those ends are.

She plays Debussy's La Mer on an ancient gramophone. There is a slight warp in the record which rises and falls, rises and falls, like the ocean. Across the esplanade Hudson's Bay rises and falls, rises and falls, like the record. It is raining on the ocean but not on the record.

Mary winds a black and silver scarf through a Matisse red dress. She brushes her hair momentarily, her hair frizzes crazily, it makes no difference whether she brushes it or not. As she brushes, she looks the nostalgic way she always looks, into the bay. The bay is her most private motif, of freedom and chance encounter, the tides of fortune or tides of love, one in the same, for her, rising and waning and rising again. The bay is her friend. They chat.

Well, she chats. The bay when it decides to speak does so by messages, bits of driftwood and weathered bottles. She has come to understand the bays language, it is like the Chinese I-Ching, except it has nothing to do with coins but with combinations of driftwood and bottles; driftwood,

driftwood, bottle, bottle, driftwood, bottle, is a message in I-Ching code. It looks like this.

```
---

---

- -

- -

---

- -
```

It is the sign of wind and water.

"It is advantageous to cross the great water, to return to the ancient temple," reads the commentary.

By which it means it is time to leave Melbourne, to go to Helsinki. Exactly as she'd planned to do, for it is an unfailing I-Ching which always tells her exactly what she wants to hear. She has already saved two thousand, seven hundred and fifty-two dollars in the Bank of Melbourne. It has just told her, she can make three dollars on a T-shirt, one dollar on a scarf, the scarves are Thai silk printed with the motif of a Thylacine. And the man Eugene can help her.

He is attracted to her.

She is attracted to him, but oh, wonders Mary, am I too old for this? Is he?

She hopes he only likes her and not more than likes her. She thinks she hopes that. She hopes she hopes that.

Mary O'Becket applies mascara thinly. She catches the ninety-six tram into the city. She'll reach the Museum at one twenty-three. At ten to two Eugene will conduct a tour of the snow-jar. She will be part of that tour. He'll have to lend her a Museum jacket, for she has forgotten hers. He'll have to help her put it on. He'll do it gallantly but clumsily. He'll want to know about the T-shirts, the ones he's seen. He'll have to think of somewhere they can talk. Mary can think of two places one is Pellegrinis, the other is, in the Observation Hide. If he asks her to Pellegrinis, it will be to sit before the long mirror where he can watch her without being obvious, which is what Pellegrinis is designed for. Naturally he'll reach the moment when he'll tell her about his wife of thirty plus years. How they don't talk any-more, how they have nothing left in common, and maybe he'll say it or maybe he'll infer it, how there is no love anymore. Men always say that, maybe it's true, maybe it's not, either way, Mary thinks, "It is their problem, not mine."

If he invites her into the snow-jar, it will mean, either he is too cheap to take her to Pellegrinis, or he's interested in what she has seen, and what she thinks of what she has seen.

Mary O'Becket dresses to look good in Pellegrinis but isn't sure which decision she prefers, Pellegrinis because it's easier or the observation hide, because she wants to be more that ogled, does she? She doesn't ask the I-Ching about Eugene, which may have been a mistake.

In the evening Mary and Eugene huddle before the Observation Hide monitors with two cups of Museum expresso. Dusk on the Tiers arrives earlier than in the Museum by a factor precisely calculated by Rosalind Son-Lee. It is growing dark now, a tint of orange in the ground mist forming over the partly frozen lakes and snowbanks. It is minus one degree celsius.

Mary whispers, "If the wolf is here it will come from the pencil-pine copses, that's where I saw it. It is very shy; we must keep still."

Mary sits with her legs tucked up on a Mersey Camp stool, a blanket draped around her. Eugene sits upright on an identical chair beside her doodling on a Thylacine Observers sheet. He watches intently. He does not expect to see the Thylacine. He has never expected to see the Thylacine, likewise he had never expected to be sitting here with Mary, and he is.

He hasn't, nor will he yet tell her of the moment many years before when he saw the real and wild *Thylacine alpina* on the real and wild Great Western Tiers. He has only ever told Nadia that, he has only ever wanted to tell Nadia. And Mary believes the Thylacine is her secret, which she can share. He likes it this way. She is sharing it wonderfully. A cautious Eugene Klein is both grateful, she has and nervous that she has. He draws question marks on the Thylacine Observers sheets and thinks of the queries which ought to precede them. The obvious, "What would Nadia think?" to the transcendental, "If, as he did, build the snow-jar so Nadia may walk back into a memory, what does it mean that Mary O'Becket has walked into the memory of Nadia Kaminski?" and finally the identical question to that which Nat asked Jeremy, "How do you know if a girl wants to kiss?"

It is dark in the snow-jar and dusk in the Museum.

Mary says, "Thank you Eugene, it was grand."

She touches him lightly on the forearm as they part at the exit. It is only then, she asks him, if she can sell her T-shirts inside the Museum.

"That way," she says, "we can talk." She smiles her most gracious smile, and as she had expected, he agrees.

From the workshop Rosalind has also been watching the monitors, waiting for the Thylacine. She has been hopeful of a sighting, the barometer is rising, the mist dispersing, usually good omens. She has begun writing a scientific paper with condescending help from Jacky, and surprisingly good advice from Martin. She needs a sighting, preferably from herself to clinch it. What she sighted this evening is Eugene and Mary, together, alone, which she finds ridiculous.

Nat would agree.

Nat would be bitterly, bitterly disappointed, for Nat thinks love, the sort of love Eugene had for Nadia, and Nadia presumably for Eugene, is eternal. Rosalind does not know if Nat is right about love, but knows at least, that Nat would agree with her both Eugene and Mary are too old for that.

Should she tell Nat?

She thinks better of it.

Should she turn off the monitors?

Should she pretend either it isn't happening, or even if it is it isn't her business?

She could have done any of these. She does none of them.

Rosalind Son-Lee alters the camera angle to read what Eugene is writing and to see if below their waists their hands are touching.

They aren't.

They do not kiss, nor do eyes meet eyes the way they do in the movies. she is glad they do not. In fact, only seven minutes later they collect their bags and leave. Rosalind quickly follows, via the short-cuts Nat has found.

Eugene and Mary nearly touch once in Progress, three times in Reptilicia, and do so in the foyer while Eugene unlocks the Museum exit.

Rosalind cannot believe it. Even if it is the slightest of touches, even if Mary did instigate it, a touch is a touch, and either one of them could have kids, grandkids her age.

As Eugene turns, he passes Rosalind crouched behind Ned Kelly's armour, and returns via Reptilicia to the snow-jar. Rosalind doesn't follow. There is a tram running in twenty minutes, enough time to either say "Adieu" or "Hurry up" to Nat and dash down the fire escape exit to Collins Street. Nat is drawing an express train winding into the Dolomite Alps, the Green Avenger and Nadia inside the wardrobe of the departing express, hiding from the Seventh Samurai, the Nazis and Rosalind presumes, the ticket inspector. The Green Avenger is rotating his hand through one hundred and eighty degrees from the wrist. He rotates his left hand, waits four frames then rotates his right hand, right then left, left then right, it is express train Tai-Chi.

Rosalind touches Nat lightly on the shoulder.

She asks, "Are you coming or staying?"

"In a minute," he says.

They will catch the forty-two tram on Collins Street to Cotham Road. Nat will ride in the open doorway. Rosalind will ride slightly behind Nat. Passing city lights along city streets they journey towards Camberwell. Rosalind hooks one leg then the other behind her knee, inventing, she says, "Tram Tai-Chi."

21. "We better talk Bud!"

Genevieve and Paul are bickering. They are in the kitchen. Nat is laying the table; he is only a room away. He cannot hear everything they are saying, but what he can hear, tells him, it is about the music room and Eugene. The room which remains choked with relics of his Great Grandfather's life, and Uncle Eugene, who remains such an unsettling influence on young Nat's life.

Genevieve says, "It isn't much to ask."

Nat wonders what is not too much to ask. If it's just the music room, then he agrees with his mother. She should have a music room. He should have a cartoon room. Uncle Eugene a map room. Joseph, a room where ghosts may visit. Nat has designed a second, a third, a fourth, a fifth and sixth story, to this house in his very private book of inventions. It is based on the Popchu Pagoda, Korea, where the Green Avenger studied the *tripikarta*, a traditional Chinese wedding cake temple, one room stacked upon another. It will begin with the music room. The second room will be Genevieve's who will not wish to be too far removed from Jeremy. The third will be Pauls for he will need to visit the lower to remember the sound of passion, and ascend to the forth to straighten out Nat. In whose room meccano sets need never be disassembled, a room to build paper-mache mountains, cardboard cities and velour seas, to fly above this paper land, on invisible fishing line, all the aeroplanes they can model and to lay over its fields and rivers, on bridges and through cuttings, a network of model train tracks. The fifth room for Eugene and his marvellous maps. The final room, of course, must be Josephs, a room for the dead.

In the fourth room of Nat's ingenious pagoda Nat will draw the Green Avenger and Nadia arguing. They have very little room to argue in the wardrobe, in the cabin, of the express train running North, but dare not risk leaving too soon. Arguments they conduct in Russian. The language of that cruel land which separates Krakow from Songkwang-sa. The irony of their respective lands, the Green Avenger once surmised is whenever we defeat the foe to our East, we do so only for the benefit of the foe on our West. That is why our lands are full of monasteries. They are also full of pig-headed men. Who will not tell Nadia of their plans.

"You do have a plan, don't you?"

"A plan," he predicted, "would unfold."

Although it is the answer she had expected, it is not under the circumstances a good answer.

Nat drew Nadia with eyes alight standing with two feet astride blocking the doorway. She says in Russian, the words Nat translates as, "We better talk bud."

Nat closes his eyes, he wants to visualize the claustrophobia. He wants to hear the blood pumping in Nadia's temples, to be able unfairly, to do the one thing you cannot do in this world, to simultaneously stare from the eyes of the Green Avenger at Nadia, and from the eyes of Nadia at the Avenger. To know what you cannot know, what each is thinking of the other. What they think is what Nat wills.

In life you cannot will your parents to stop their bickering about, what is only a room in a house full of rooms. Or will his father say over asparagus and cream that it is time to begin the building of the pagoda in Nat's very private book of inventions, so each of us who comprise this family can have their room to dream. Nat can neither will nor know what each of his parents think as they numbly pass the potatoes.

What Genevieve thinks is simply to wish that she did not have to bicker or plea, that Paul could just once understand her point of view.

What Paul wonders is why Eugene had so easily escaped all the responsibilities of life.

PART 4.

The Society of the Wolf

Melbourne Age December 1983
The Dambusters…. Starring Almost Everyone.

Confrontation on the Gordon River, approximately 70 "Greenies" camped near the construction site of the Gordon below Franklin dam dressed in everything from coloured flags to long johns confronted police and HEC workers witnessed by 50 reporters, photographer's and cameramen. A confrontation reminiscent of a Hollywood movie or circus performance, complete with rafts and riverboats, flags and battens.

Police have arrested a number of protesters who will be summarily charged and transported to Hobart to await trial. A Hydro Electricity Commission spokesman has asks the protesters not join this exercise in futility which will only escalate the tensions.

22. Join Now.

In the third tent in the foyer of Mersey Camp, Gallery Five, Mary O'Becket begins her T-shirt sales. She has added some new lines; a Thylacine motif drawn in the primitive X-ray fashion, various Society of the Wolf T-shirts, where a yin and yan circle is formed partly by a stylized wolf and partly by the lettering, numerous scarfs, T-towels and postcards. Mary O'Becket loves postcards, she loves receiving them with stamps bearing unreadable graphic alphabets and with tiny cryptic messages from Zoey. Mary sent a Society of the Wolf postcard to Zoey in Helsinki with the words;

"Join now!"

Written in blood red texta. She prints both postcard and message poster size and hangs them in her peddlers' tent.

On July twenty seven, someone does, join now.

Her name is Di Jacobson. She stands in the flapway of the tent with her Observers sheet filled in and wearing a Museum jacket over a pair of men's overalls tie-dyed orange.

She asks, "Where do I?"

Mary wonders what.

"Where do I join? The society, where do I join the Society of the Wolf."

Mary has to admit she isn't sure, since, "if you join, you'll be the very first member." If she joins, the society of the wolf will cease to be a joke, it would become an entity. Entities need cards, nicely printed cards, they need bumper stickers and wall posters and, as Di Jacobson suggests, a president.

"Okay," says Mary, "You're president."

The president proposed, The Society of the Wolf authoritively ask Mary if she would like a cup of what passes for coffee in this Museum and equally decisively goes to fetch it. Mary figures on a pocket calculator if a package of T-shirt, membership card, bumper sticker and poster could be incorporated into a membership fee to return a small profit. The answer in seven simple steps is, "yes". She costs three rates of membership; the student, the supporter, and the sponsorship, each with its own colour T-shirt and card. The president says, "What a perfectly lovely idea." The president says, she thinks she is going to like being president, she has never been president of anything before, and the first act of a president will be to increase the membership in order that she be president of someone other than herself. "The road to success is a straight line", is her motto. Whatever the motto is meant to mean, Di Jacobson interpreted it as an excuse to bang on anyone's door with whatever issue has aroused her passion. Today's passion is the Thylacine.

"The world must know."

Di Jacobson had spoken for forty-seven minutes to Stan "Scoop" Munro in the *Herald Sun* press room, and twenty minutes in the observation hide, by the time the exhibit is closed to the public and Mary met Eugene in the now deserted hide.

Mary wears a patchwork quilted Jacket, she didn't print herself, while Eugene wears his much-travelled duffle-coat, with the small cloth emblems, Mount Buffalo, Eden, and Hastings Caves, Tasmania, stitched on the sleeve. They have lugged camp stools from base camp, Mersey River and unfold them before the television screens. Mary notes the weather on the Tiers in appropriate boxes on the Thylacine Observer's sheet she has clipped into a loose-leaf folder. The conditions are not good, a wind has sprung, it is blustering snow cluttered mist through the pencil-pine and over the lake. They watch each consecutive snow squall as it dusts across the ice.

"Like a breath," she smiles, "from the grey-haired god of the wind."

Two hours earlier, although neither Eugene nor Mary are aware two adult Thylacines had played chasey on the ice. Thirty-seven eye-witnesses crammed the monitors, one of whom was Stan "Scoop" Munro.

Neither Mary nor Paul were interested at that moment to know what Stan "Scoop" Munro had seen. They are too interested in each other.

23. The worth of a Dot.

The *Melbourne Herald* reports, "Much Agog about the Dog", the *Melbourne Age*, "A wolf Snarls its Critics". Henk Van Der Sarr clutches both articles as he addresses the first gathering of his team in conference room three, Zoological Buildings.

"The Museum is lying."

He pauses, he draws a handkerchief from his breast pocket, removes his spectacles and quickly wipes them. Re-pockets his handkerchief but does not place his spectacles back on his nose, rather he uses them to gesture into space.

"This is unfortunate."

He lowers his voice. "The truth, when we find it may not gather headlines. We are not in the headline business. Nor are we in the myth making business. You are in the business of facts, and I am in the business of energy."

The "you" he refers to has gathered under the auspices of the Subcommittee responsible for Expeditions {Zoological}, to consider the possibility of mounting a search for the Tiger Wolf. The photographs have disappeared, replaced by a set of one to ten thousand scale contour maps, a set of cameras, and a statement of the known facts. The statement is conservative, it is precise, it is the facts as Jacky would have expressed them. They are, asserts Henk Van Der Sarr, the point of agreement.

He drew their attention to the largest of the cameras. It photographs in the infra-red range, the spectrum of heat, and by implication of life. The camera is expensive, it is a very large black box, used according to Henk Van Der Sarr in aerial photography. He shows them a photograph taken by this camera, it is not of the wolf, it was taken over the Kruger National Park, South Africa, it is a photograph of dots, constellations of dots, where each dot is a wildebeest.

"One thousand two hundred and twenty-seven dots, to be precise. It is very easy to find one thousand wildebeest, not so easy to find a single Thylacine."

He displays a second camera. It is very small, and very cheap. The photograph it has taken is snapshot size. The photograph was taken here, at the Melbourne Zoo, in the wolf enclosure at night, a photograph of the heat a wolf makes pacing. While the image is recognizably a wolf, the heat signature alone, Henk Van Der Sarr explains, would have identified it. The camera range is short, barley three metres, its operation by trip-wire it is therefore critical to have many cameras and a strategy.

"I have both."

Henk's strategy consists of a transparent grid sheet laid over the one to ten thousand contour map of the Great Pine Tier, and based on the first principle, nature is not random, and a second more adventurous presumption that the reason people do not find something is either they look in the wrong place or they do not know, what the thing they seek, looks like.

"About the Thylacine we know neither."

His strategy is to install the infra-red cameras in a manner which presumes nothing. To this end he will need a team, a dedicated, specialist team under the auspices of the Zoological Society, but who will, he assures them be supported abundantly, both tactically and scientifically, by the H.E.C. Special Projects.

"The Commission does not like loose ends, they have a habit of unravelling the best laid plans."

He did not explain how the wolf had become a loose end but explained in minute detail the strategy of placing infra-red cameras on the Tiers. His strategy came down to a choice between the letters Y and Z, written in gigantic scale across that landscape of ice.

Harold Nicholson brushes his fingers through a trim reddish beard, proposing the capital letter Y. He envisages the tail will extend the length of the Lake Sidon Valley, the twin V's on the Fish River and Wild Dog Creek respectively.

Col Stewart advances the letter Z, with the top right tip at Solomon's Jewels, the first buckle above Lake Sidon camp, the diagonal rising onto the Walls of Jerusalem and the lower horizontal on the high south sloping and bitterly exposed Damascus Tier.

Jacky will accept a commission in this team, however uneasy Henk Van Der Sarr made her feel, she knew she would accept. It is everything, of course, she has dreamt of but not immediately, and not before searching for whatever information she can gather on Henk Van Der Sarr and his Hydro Electricity Commission. She expects to find very little. She finds nothing which will change her mind.

They will cross the straight to Tasmania on August eighteen, arrive on the Tiers August twenty one.

24. In which Rosalind, Jacky, and Mary are perplexed.

Mary asks Eugene, "Is this how you remember it?"

They sit in their usual coats, in their usual stools but now without even the semblance of a gap between them. "Yes", he answers, "of course it would be larger if we were there, but if we were there rather than here, we would still be watching the snow fall as it is, in sheets down the Vales, the clouds would bank exactly as they do along the escarpments and the wind would puff snow banks back into the sky the way it is doing it just over there near the Lake bank. And you and I would be colder than we are, especially our feet and our hands and the tips of our noses."

"But," she touches him lightly on the arms, "we would be somewhere else, a long way away."

And it would seem, oh so natural there rather than here, to take that next bothersome step. The "do you love me?" "Yes, I do." "Do you want to lay with me?" Touch me gently, kiss my lips, why, oh why, do we do this?

Into the landscape of Mary O'Beckets longing, Jacky Lambert trudges long squelching steps in fresh, sodden snow. They had risen steeply from Mersey River; misty rain became misty snow at one thousand metres. Snow which melts as it lands on the shoulders, lands on the cap and lands on the rucksack of a lanky Harold Nicholson trudging ahead.

"Snow," says their guide, "I love how it smells like steel."

Their guide breaths deeply, once, twice, three times, he is lightly dressed despite the snow, wearing the cap of his native Bavaria, a course woollen shirt and knee length climbing breeches. While his party sits zipping coats and dropping rucksacks, Henrick either jumps or jogs where he stands, announcing.

"We travel one hundred and two degrees east south east following the Zion Vale, maybe sometimes we do not see very much but lost we will not become."

They will rise a further two hundred and fifty metres clearing the tree line in one hundred metres altitude and two kilometres horizontal distance. They will not become lost. And even though both Jacky and Harold had, disguised as the public, seen the Museums replica of the Great Western Tiers through the windows and the consuls of Eugene Klein's snow-jar. The Tiers they now venture into is not everything they expected, it is everything and more.

They expect the wind.

How it whines in the high escarpments descending in ebbies to the passes they trudge.

They expect the mist.

Dense and unrelenting.

They expect that the snow-gum forest they squat in will cease once they rise one hundred metres in altitude.

And it does.

They expect the alpine heath which will replace it, the gorged escarpments and glacial lakes, the few pencil-pine copses, the scree beneath the cliff faces. And they expect the gaiter deep cover of fresh fallen snow.

What they do not expect is the whiteness, or how much the whiteness fills them with fear, but of what they cannot say.

Into that whiteness, they climb, descend, zig-zag, skirt, semi-frozen lakes and icy escarpments until late in the evening they pitch amongst the pencil-pine and pandanus of a lake Sidon shore their Sidon Base Camp, for lost, they did not become. Henrick Kohl and Col Stewart will retrace this journey and return five times in ten days to stock the Lake Sidon camp. While over ice crusted ground Harold and Jacky will survey the Zee, like Zorro. The pattern they have agreed the cameras will take. On the Tiers proper they tread warily wearing instep crampons, spikes strapped to their boots. Along the Damascus Vale escarpment, buffered by mist, "where," suggests Harold, "a wolf would be crazy to go". But the wolf would not be crazy, he notes, to venture into the high heath banking Solomon's Jewels or to go beneath the protected eastern wall of the Temple, where within picture postcard pines Harold skis poorly and Jacky elegantly down to find, "wolf tracks?". Jacky measures with a calibrator, width and depth, she notes in a black spiral bound notebook how little they differ from the plaster cast found long ago by Rosalind Son-Lee.

What is, she wonders, that audacious girl doing, as they turn north between the Temple and Mount Jerusalem's escarpment to the Lake Sidon camp. Cloud hanging low and grey and beginning to snow as the late afternoon temperature plummets.

It plummets on the monitors as Anita Graige directs the television crew onto the Observation Hide to interview Martin McKenzie, its creator.

"Now they have gone too far, much too far."

Rosalind is het up, she has run up from the snow-jar where a television crew has begun setting up its cameras. Anita Graige in the role of media liaison girl stands beside Martin McKenzie who jokes with the interviewer.

"Videos will become the fossils of the twenty-first century and this dome its prototype zoo."

Anita Graige smiles, they film her gorgeous white teeth, and record Martin's joke. It is the statement they wanted, the pun they desire, one single sentence and half a minute of film.

Nat had just finished drawing his hero, confronting the villain, face to face, eye to eye. Neither had blinked, neither flinched nor had spoken, exactly how it should be in a fight to the death. He was in the grandest of moods before Rosalind interrupts him with a rage sprung from nowhere, he can't comprehend.

"I don't think they care. I just don't think they care Nat."

She is standing beside the doorway, her feet astride, the muscles beneath her eyes are twitching.

"Is that all you are going to do Nat, play with your cartoon?"

Rosalind turns to leave, to go somewhere, but she cannot think, just then, of where that somewhere may be. She cannot return to the Observation Hide with the television cameras focussing their attention on Martin. She cannot return to the Society of the Wolf tent since yesterday Mary winked vulgarly at Elizabeth, {can you believe it? Elizabeth has joined the Society of the Wolf}, suggesting that her and Nat are boyfriend and girlfriend, or something even more seamy. Boyfriend and girlfriend, they have no right to say that. She cannot go and visit Eugene for she cannot look Nat's uncle in the face knowing what she does about Mary. And she cannot go where mostly she wishes, for Jacky has departed to the Tiers. She goes where she knows, nobody will browse, on the things she believes are her own. She goes to the diggings. She scales the first ladder, follows the second and the third over the chaos of storeroom into the heart of the digs. There is nothing she expects to find. Yet there may be something, something small, something which didn't appear significant in the headlong rush to find the film.

There isn't.

25. Eugene tells the truth.

"What was it like?" once whispered Nadia.

"Please tell me," Mary now asks.

Elizabeth had told Mary, how Rosalind had told her, how Nat had told Rosalind, what Eugene had told Joseph and Joseph told Jon who would tell his daughter in law who would one day tell Nat, about the long-ago moment, back in Eugene's childhood, when he stood on the lake shore, watching the wolf.

"You didn't tell me," She touches him momentarily, hand to hand, "Why?"

Eugene sits forward looking into the closest television consul, his head trussed by a triangle of both arms, resting his chin on his thumbs, the way children pray.

"It used to be a kind of secret. I didn't tell Nat, Genevieve did. And I didn't tell Genevieve, Jon did. I told Nadia, that's the only person I ever told."

The only Nadia Mary O'Becket knew is a cartoon character in the "The New Adventures of the Green Avenger". Mary doesn't need to be told that the two Nadia's, although related, are not the same person. Nor does she need to be told the significance of Nadia, there is a sadness and a tone some men reserve for their one tragic love. Eugene is the one tragic love kind of person. It's why she likes him.

"Was she beautiful?"

"In her way."

"How long did you know her?"

"It was in the war when time was different, so much more intense. We were lucky we had what time we did."

"Did she die?"

Did she die? Eugene doesn't really know. He thinks she did. He thinks she must have, given where she went, and when. She could not have survived, no one could have.

"I think she probably did."

"But you didn't look?"

"No."

"You should have looked Gene."

Europe was in ruins. He didn't know where she may have been sent. Poland, on the Russian side? Poland was smashed, flattened by ten thousand-pound incendiary bombs, night raid after bloody night raid. He knew, he dropped them. You couldn't find anything in that mess. He doesn't say that to Mary. For the first time in his life he tells someone the truth.

"I didn't have the faith to look."

Neither Mary nor Eugene spoke for one long squall of snow falling across the monitors.

Mary spoke first.

"There is a fire, a fire on Lake Sidon. It must be for us."

26. In which Nat discovers the Truth.

There is a fire beside which Jacky Lambert stamps shivering feet, as she sips hot cocoa from a plastic mug while Harold Nicholson jokes at their alpine idyllic scene, the lake, the pines, the fire crackling and the solitude.

Every evening on a Lake Sidon shore the same fire burns. It burns for Mary's desire as it burns for Rosalind's misgivings.

"What is it doing there?" She asks.

And every answer smack of quasi science, forth dimensional trickery or E.S.P. The model is behaving unreasonably. The model is going beyond its parameters.

Rosalind wants to know why.

She admits she designed the program under pressure, that the film and the journals and Eugene's enormous multicoloured map were all so dangerously subjective. It is possible, either Nat's drawings or the film accidently programmed Joseph, an image of Joseph, his shadow perhaps into the program thus into the snow-jar. It is possible the fire is Josephs that he's sitting near it cooking his spuds. It is possible, just ridiculous. It therefore follows, given the subjective nature of their original input and Nat's considerable stupidity that either Joseph or Eugene has also been programmed into the dome. And what if Eugene enters the snow-jar as an eleven-year-old boy, what would Eugene think of Eugene in a time loop? It is of course possible, may even be likely, but what Rosalind wonders would such a thing mean. And how much Rosalind wonders will people blame her. And how Rosalind wonders can she put it back right?

On this Sunday evening Rosalind watches the figure of a man in long "dry as a bone" coat and slouch hat for two long minutes on Lake Sidon banks.

On this Sunday evening Rosalind panics.

She shows Nat.

She forgot about Mary and Eugene.

She should have turned those monitors off, she should have at least thought of that. Once he'd looked, even though he doesn't at first notice the spy monitor, she couldn't turn it off, without alerting his attention. Nat looks at the weather update, the long scan , the close ups in an order which has become professional.

He has his own theory about the figure inside, which he begins to tell Rosalind.

"It is," he begins to elaborate, "the nature......"

It is then that Nat notices Mary, then that he notices Eugene.

He looks at Rosalind who is blushing and he knows that she knows and has known for some time. Nat feels betrayed, by Rosalind, by Eugene, who ought, who must, who can do nothing else, but remain forever faithful to his one tragic love, for that is the nature of romantic adventure. And anyway, they are too old for love.

Rosalind does not speak. She doesn't know the grown-up words to say. Nat doesn't expect Rosalind to. Somehow, he hopes Jeremy will.

Nat lies in bed waiting for Jeremy to finish playing a Mendelssohn lullaby, the last piece for the night, but every-time he makes a mistake he must begin again. Nat closes his eyes, he pretends with more than the normal venom, he is a Messerschmitt pilot dive bombing from out of the ceiling, twelve o'clock high. Down, down, down, on the unsuspecting bulk of his Great Uncles Lancaster. His guns open up, tracers passing the tip of the bombers tail wing. He straightens out alert for fighters, rat-a-tat tat, rat-a-tat tat, Nat banks to the right rising steeply, rolls, and with pure finesse blasts the Spitfire out of the sky. He turns on the now unescorted Lancaster, rat-a-tat tat, rat-a-tat tat, dropping on its tail, again and again, until in blinding flash, the bomber explodes.

Jeremy has finally finished the lullaby. He will pack up his music sheets, say "Goodnight" to their mother and swagger up the stairs to their room. Even before he reaches the door Nat's body is trembling. When Jeremy enters he doesn't say anything.

He cannot.

He practices mouthing sounds until sounds return while Jeremy twists and turns, and when he knows it will come out truly he tells Jeremy what is foremost on his mind.

"I'm running away."

"Where?" Jeremy whispers excitedly.

"Where do you think?"

"How could I know?"

"Into the Tiers."

27. In which Nat and Rosalind hatch a Plan.

"How?" Rosalind asks.

"Through the window."

"What will be in there?"

"Rocks and ice."

"When?"

"As soon as I've packed."

"I have to come too."

"If you promise not to trip."

They shake their secret handshake and kiss their secret kiss.

It will take five days to collect the essentials on Nat's long and elaborate list. The list begins with the words, "What is this?" which Rosalind appreciates means nothing at all, but Nat claims is the Green Avengers mantra. The first item, rucksacks, Nat drew, because they couldn't be any ordinary rucksack, one must be the rucksack in Jeremy's cupboard, the second the rucksack on level C5 of storage room R, which is where Nat found the first.

The tent, he also drew, is the tent of ghosts in the moving picture, The Ascent of Mount Jerusalem directed by his Great Grandfather. It is Nat understood manufactured by the firm, "Blacks of Greenock" and can be purchased in Elsternwick. Nat will go on Wednesday. Sleeping bags, they can borrow, one from Jeremy, one from Elizabeth. There is a spirit burning camp stove and a compass of his grandfather's in the static displays, both of which they will also borrow. Boots, they will need boots and snow shoes if possible. Where, oh where, Nat wonders has he last seen snow-shoes. He sits beside Rosalind on a homeward tram, holding hands behind their bums, in case a prefect sees, while Nat lists aloud all the places he could have seen snow-shoes. Jeremys top drawer, his own top drawer, in the cartoon room, in the workshop or the monitor room, no, it was longer ago than that it must have been in the storerooms, in the Klein Bequest.

"No." says Rosalind, "there are no snow-shoes with the Bequest."

"But of course," smiles Nat. "with the crevasse ladders in storeroom A."

Climbing breeches and anoraks they will find clothing the mannequins, Scot and Oats, in a now defunct static display titled, "Antarctica, the Last Adventure."

The list, Nat explains is no accident, for if the list is followed to the letter, they will look identical to the two figures on a Lake Sidon shore seventy years ago. They must look identical or the programme will reject them.

Elizabeth cannot believe Rosalind when she rings her that night.

"You can't."

"You are."

"When."

"No."

"Have you thought about sleeping?"

"Not sleeping, sleeping, silly, sleeping with Nat."

She hadn't exactly thought about it, not rationally. She had, "fancies" which sometimes embarrasses her. Not so much for what she fancied she is doing, but for her longing, how unscientific it is. And how it can exist within her, this mood she cannot comprehend. It will be easier, far easier to enter the snow-jar than to enter that silly-girl part of her mind. They will enter the snow-jar on a Friday at five twenty through window number seven. Rosalind will enter first, Nat will pass the rucksacks through, then follow, before they re-seal the window.

The heroic land is a quiet land, a cold and silent land, but not at all an unfamiliar land. It is a land where fear is the most favourite of fears and freedom the most alarming.

28. Not all is Revealed.

The I-Ching has been loafing. Every night Mary has walked where the waves wash bone white onto the shore picking up the most likely sticks and bottles and reading their patterns. It should have foretold everything which happened in the days which followed Nat's vanishing, when it foretold nothing at all.

It did not foretell, Nat and Rosalind prying open window seven and entering the snow-jar.

It did not foretell, Genevieve throwing Eugene from her house, not to return until he returns her son from his stupid invention and throwing everything of Josephs from her music room onto the neatly mown, front lawn.

It did not foretell, Mary finding Eugene sleeping in the Society of the Wolf tent on the camp bed belonging to his father. And it did not foretell, Eugene kissing Mary when she laughs. She should not really have laughed.

In the third day of Nat and Rosalind's disappearance the I-Ching would far no better.

29. Who Knew.

"Who Knew?" Genevieve can't believe, Nat tells Jeremy everything. "You must have known." But, "No," he lies he didn't. He didn't really, really know, and it's better in this state, not to tell his mother.

His mother's ranting, his mother's mad, furious with Eugene who should not have come back from the war, how dare he live when others died, other's so much better. There are so many "ifs" to ask, if only Joseph's father not taken Joseph to that bloody lake to watch the wild wolves bounding, if only Joseph had thought to live a quite live like others did, a lawyer or accountant. If only Eugene had married her, whoever she was anyway, and turned the head of another boy, Nat's been difficult from the start, all bound up in his own weird world. If only Paul had spent more time getting to know his second son. If only Eugene hadn't lived in the house, which by rights is his. And do not think she doesn't know all about that Chinese girl, she has a part in this as well, encouraging the stupid boy.

She is going to go there, speak her piece to any one who'll listen. In the foyer, by the tents, Mersey Camp and the Tiers, while she huffed and puffed that they had confused their history, the spectacles which Joseph wore he didn't even wear then, and where on earths the gramophone, she loved that story most of all, to walk in circles to a waltz upon a stage of ice and snow, that at least she understands. She doesn't understand at all; a Society of the Wolf, the giant map which Eugene made, where on your map is my son? She didn't understand the screens, the view of ice and snow and wind. And she began to wonder if, she really knew who her son was; a thought that seeps into her soul.

Genevieve Klein misses by fifteen minutes and fifteen hours; the simultaneous sightings of the wolf on Lake Sidon shore and the figure in black silk robes on Lake Sidon banks. To have witnessed that she would have had to sat with the members of the Society of the Wolf, during their salute to the night, welcoming the end of another day on the Tiers, another moment in the life of the white wolf, another revelation from their hero, Dr Seon, sitting in meditation posture in the black silk cape of the Green Avenger, whistling for the wolf.

PART 5.

In a Distant Place

Melbourne Age January 1982
It's On for One and All!

"Greenie" numbers keep increasing on the Gordon River camp, in the Queenstown lock-up and in the Hobart Goal, as the battle for the Gordon River shows no sight of abating. Bob Brown of the Wilderness Society, was the latest protestor arrested in the most well-mannered arrest imaginable. Bob Brown, elegant in shirt and tie, shook hands with the representative of the H.E.C. and joked with police officers during his arrest.

Confrontations at the dam site on the Gordon River are now almost daily and show no sign of abating. It has become the "Cause Celebrate" for this generation of dreadlocked hippies.

30. Sutra.

Ever since Nat Klein began wearing the black silk cape of the Green Avenger, this journey has taken on the appearance of a holy quest.

Rosalind and Nat, rucksack laden, treading laboriously, on ice crusted snow-shoes over a featureless landscape. Rosalind plotting a proudly accurate course with Nat's pocket compass across Eugene's graded blue lines of doubt and certainty. She plots their own course in pencil, their companions in red biro. Their companions are wolves. They had first noticed them this morning and have been following them ever since. a young pair, wolf like around the face, but not in their gait, which resembles a trot, light fawn in colour with the distinctive tiger stripes across their rump and extending along their backs.

The wolves do not disappoint Rosalind Son-Lee.
The wolves remain at the edge of their vision, usually ahead, sometimes to the right, sometimes to the left, where three sightings occur concurrently to either right or left, Rosalind shifts their course in the appropriate direction. Their direction is, west south west.

Their direction leads them across a ridge of five rocks. The rocks are not polystyrene, they are the only five authentic rocks in the snow-jar, Nat knows, he put them there. With Martin McKenzie's help, they'd lifted them into place, out of a Melbourne City Council wheelbarrow, lent to the

Museum in April nineteen fifty-four. They'd placed the dolomite boulders amongst the polystyrene, two parallel ridges Martin had dubbed, maxi-ridge and mini-ridge. When the snow fell on June the thirteenth it covered the mini-ridge within the first seven hours, except for a single protruding quartz-ite boulder, five dolomite boulders mark the maxi-ridge. Nat and Rosalind have crossed this ridge ninety-seven times since they entered the snow-jar.

The first eleven times Nat believed they were travelling in ceaseless tight circles of a Chopin waltz. Rosalind could not convince him otherwise, not by showing him the readings on his very own pocket compass, nor the pencil marks across the multi-coloured map. And although she concedes the scratches on the ridge top ice suggest they are travelling repeatedly, across the same ridges the science of compass and map doesn't lie.

The twelfth time they'd crossed the ridge top Nat has asked Rosalind where they are going.

He asked her again one hour later. He thought it was a good idea, to keep in touch.

"Mount Jerusalem", she'd said the first time.

"Jaffa Vale," she'd said the second, they'd veered slightly to the south, evidently enough to miss Mount Jerusalem.

She points this out on compass and map.

Rosalind Son-Lee has flakes of fresh snow on a navy-blue balaclava, drib-lets of melted snow on her spectacle lenses. She coaxes a smile from beneath a black silk scarf, balaclava and jacket hood. The smile constrained by the folds of the fabrics and the timidness of the author, like all Rosalind Son-Lee smiles. Nat believes they are like lost pieces of Chinese calligraphy, intrigu-ing, enigmatic and distant.

Enigmatic, in Rosalind's eyes, is Nat wearing the black silk jacket of the Green Avenger, and his whistling, what Nat calls, the wolf sutra.

"A sutra," Rosalind explains, "is a sacred Buddhist chant, not some silly made up whistle."

Nat's sutra is one long whistle followed by a pause of exactly fifteen heart-beats, a short whistle of seven beats, another pause, another seven. It serves no conceivable purpose. It would serve no conceivable purpose even if it was a sutra. According to Rosalind, it is Nat trying to be metaphysical, it is sheer coincidence only that Nat's whistling of the wolf sutra coincided exactly with the sighting of the wolf. Rosalind is certain about this, anything else would be pseudo-science, E.S.P. or something equally unfounded.

Rosalind ignored the coincidence and busied herself taking notes. Rosalind has, to Rosalind's pride, already filled five pages, in careful handwriting, on a quarto pad. She had noted precisely, the conditions at o-seven hundred hours as Nat tugged on the cape of the Green Avenger and began his sutra.

It was still. It was neither raining nor snowing. It was clear. It was a very cold minus five degrees celsius on Nat's not particularly accurate maximum minimum thermometer. What the snow-jar monitors read at exactly that moment Rosalind would have loved to have known. The snow-jar monitors she trusts.

She'd noted, correctly, it was a bitter morning to do so senseless a thing as, just sit. She'd noted, at what moment, {but not on which whistle} the tiger-wolves appeared. Out of the mist, one pair trotting. She'd noted how they'd paused, one hundred metres away, ears alert, sniffing. How, when they'd moved, they'd done so, tardily casting eyes backwards.

Nat and Rosalind then began their pursuit of the wolves. Nat and Rosalind cannot travel quickly, their rucksacks are heavy, their snow shoes clumsy. Rosalind jots this down. She has recorded everything since the night, two nights ago, when they pried the window from the snow-jar and entered.

Rosalind entered first, following her rucksack onto the ice beneath the window. The cold had surprised her. Minus seven degrees celsius had meant little on the monitors compared to how cold it feels on your toes, on your nose or the crackly tips of Rosalind Son-Lee's ear lobes.

Nat followed through the window, with his plan, a simple plan to journey just far enough away to be out of range of the cameras. Over the ridge and down in the dale, somewhere near the lake shore, somewhere near the pines. Nat led, carrying his projector torch, sweeping the beam, through white mist, in a direction he only knew as, "that-a-way". A scant torchlight beam is not beam enough to distinguish between whiteness that is ice and whiteness that is mist. {It is strange how fearful the whiteness can be.} Rosalind stumbled but did not trip. She'd promised not to trip.

That first night they had camped "somewhere". Rosalind described that somewhere as flattish and white. They camped in the Blacks of Greenock tent which Nat claimed he could pitch in three minutes flat. He pitched it in five minutes and fifty-seven seconds. She wrote that down too.

Elizabeth Kylie's final advice to Rosalind about boys and Nat is was to zip her sleeping bag eight inches above her navel, to wear track suit pants, and night shirt with buttons, to talk until Nat starts yawning and only to let him kiss you once he's promised you his heart or something else equally as silly.

It was minus seven degrees celsius the first night in the Blacks of Greenock tent. Rosalind Son-Lee wore every article of clothing she'd carried and huddled beside Nat, who talked until she slept.

He spoke of his Great Grandfather. The man Nat knew was a very old man, a very frail man, with hair which was almost transparent and eyes as pale as talc. "He didn't need his eyes anymore because he could see absolutely everything without them. He would train himself, he claimed, by remembering a day, perhaps a day many years ago in Krakow. He would challenge me, his day in Krakow, my yesterday in Camberwell. We would ask each other questions. What was the street name where you saw Steven Wilson? Who was sitting immediately behind you in kindergarten? What colour hair did the waiter, the young waiter in the Jagiellonian university cafe have, red or brown? You weren't allowed to cheat, and anyway it didn't matter because no one ever won, and no one ever lost."

"I showed him my first film although he was already blind. When it was over he asked me, "Is there more or less colour on the wall or on the slide?" That question astonished me, and I still don't know the answer, although I think it must be the same. if there is more colour on the wall, where did it come from? If there is less colour, where did it go?" Rosalind lay huddled beside him breathing chill clouds of vapour. She thought the answer obvious, once you substituted light for colour, since there is only one source of light in his Grandfather's puzzle, the "Eveready" flashlight which guided them to wherever here is. Surprisingly she didn't tell Nat that. She was too tired. They woke simultaneously with a query on their lips, an open the tent flaps and look outside query.

They expected a roof. There was no roof.

They expected walls. There were no walls.

There was an expanse of ice, low ridges lakes and ice, exactly as they had painted them on the inside of the snow-jar walls.

"It looks," said Nat, "so real."

Their tent was pitched, awkwardly, on a gentle incline against a low ridge of boulders. The pine copse, their destination, to the not so-distant northeast, banking the partly frozen lake. In the afternoon Nat would descend to the lake, all morning he would help Rosalind establish her hides amongst the ridges of the snow-jar, the hides they would man in the evening and early morning according to Rosalind's roster. Early the second morning, this morning, Nat didn't man his hide, he whistled. He whistled from a snow bank above their new encampment amongst the pines, he whistled low and wee and two grey Thylacines came running.

It wasn't good science. It hasn't been good science since Nat put on the jacket of the Green Avenger.

31. In which the Wind begins to Blow.

At exactly two fifteen on the second day of their quest the land began to change. It had been rising slowly all morning, now suddenly, to the north and south west it began falling steeply. The wolves veer to the left.

"Jaffa…Vale."

Rosalind points it out, illustrated on his Eugene's map in handsome Prussian Blue, number thirty-five in Nat's Derwent pencil box. The colour Nat drew the interior of the Vienna express in the last frame he completed before Rosalind and he entered the snow-jar. It was a good frame, full of dramatic tension. The Seventh Samurai gesturing to Nadia and the Green Avenger, that they share his table. Neither Nat nor the Avenger knew exactly, what was about to happen next. Should the Green Avenger kill the Seventh Samurai? Will the Seventh Samurai kill the Green Avenger? Will either use the tried and true poison in the coffee cup passing through the tunnel routine, or is that too corny? Rosalind would think it's too corny. So, does Nadia. Not just corny but downright embarrassing, neither she nor Nadia Kaminski want to be cast in such a role. It is this rather than the wolf, which Nat thinks about as they cross the ninety-seven ridges of ice on the way to Jaffa Vale.

He'd brought a small box of pencils, some wax paper frames, if he thought of a solution, he could draw it.

He didn't, and the land began to change.

The plateaux fractures, gorged by paths of ancient ice, ploughing a mountain here, a valley there, cirque lakes cased by pines. Into Jaffa Vale the procession descends. Jaffa Vale, the full-stop of Col Stewart's Z, crisscrossed by tripwires, saturated by infra-red cameras. Rosalind activates two simply by unclogging her snow shoes. Nat is snapped glissading down a low fast gully of snow, and camera V26, finally catches a Thylacine trotting assuredly through the pines.

The cameras record; Nat Klein erecting his Blacks of Greenock tent in a record four minutes and fifteen seconds, Rosalind Son-Lee warming herself beside a small pine bone fire, facing it, turning her back to it, seventeen times. The cameras don't record, this night the temperature fell to a comparatively mild plus four degrees. Rosalind did not wear her balaclava, scarf, or woollen polo neck jumper to bed. She wore the night shirt Elizabeth had recommended, buttoned to the second button, a spencer beneath. She unzips her sleeping bag to eight inches above her navel, unzips Nat's, so his arms can reach into where her hands lay twitching, loose cotton on her sleeping bag seam. Nat touches Rosalind on the left index finger, inside the cocoon of her sleeping bag, inside the Blacks of Greenock tent, beneath the Jaffa Vale night.

No prefect saw.

No dobber told.

He touches her forth, then third finger and the piece of cotton twine she has twisted around her second. Still no prefect saw, no camera snaps. A place secret enough to kiss, tongue to tongue, the grown-up way. To tentatively approach the uncharted territory beneath Rosalind's spencer.

"Mmm," she whispers as he kisses a nipple, "It's tingley, like Life Savers."

He lay in his sleeping bag, on her sleeping bag. This is tingley too, in another denser way, but Rosalind is too embarrassed to think of another analogy, and anyway she doesn't need an analogy to tell her it feels gushy.

This far, and no more, exactly as instructed.

"I'm not ready yet, to go you know, too far, you do understand Nat." Nat nods.

Nat understands.

He understands, "not ready", in the thumping of his own heart and the trembling of his fingers.

Nat also understands, or believes he understands much more than he did as they crawled through the window. He understands that either he, his Great

93

Grandfather, or Rosalind Son-Lee had invented the *Thylacine alpina*; that they are following it across a land they also invented, to a destination they cannot know. He understands when he wears the cape of the Green Avenger he feels courage, not in his soul, where courage ought to be felt but in his sleeves, and whatever it is, that he whistles, the wolves believe, it is a sutra. He understands, it felt delicious to kiss the left nipple of Rosalind Son-Lee, and that sooner or later more deliciousness will follow. But he doesn't understand where the line should lie between what we are ready for and what we are not, and he doesn't understand how they will ever find the window again.

If Jacky Lambert and Harold Nicholson had begun their routine camera check along the top of the Z, towards Solomon's Jewels, instead of beginning at the full stop which marks its base, they may, or may not have met Rosalind and Nat. An encounter which would have created grave difficulties with Rosalind Son-Lee's perception of space and time. Fortunately, they began at the full-stop which marks their vast Z's base. Nat and Rosalind packed camp at the centre of the full stop at about the same time Jacky and Harold left Lake Sidon. Jacky and Harold entered Jaffa Vale via Jaffa Gate as Nat and Rosalind exited via Damascus gate. Their chance to witness each other, across the U of the glacial valley, obscured by mist.

The wolves had returned on schedule and in tune early this morning. They began a lively trot, east, north-east, rising steeply towards the west col of the U-shaped valley. Mist obscures their vision beyond a few hundred metres, dense low cloud covers the higher peaks. At exactly nine thirty-seven according to Rosalind's notes snow begins falling, and falling, and falling.

Jacky and Harold reach the first infra-red camera as the weather begins to deteriorate, the camera J26, with the one true photo of the Thylacine. It is the only image they retrieve, as prudently, they decide to retreat. Ten minutes later Nat suggests to Rosalind by the Pool of Bethesda, that they pitch at nine forty-five in the morning, their haven for that night, and the next night, and the next night.

The wind began to blow.

The wind blew sixteen inches of ice and rock off the summit of King David's peak and deposited them on the orange Blacks of Greenock tent. It blew the entire contents of the Pool of Bethesda onto its northern bank, where it hung in a white wall defying gravity. It blew every tip of every pine copse tree into the ice before it, prayerful, devout. It blew the brand-new aluminium pole which centres the Black's tent into an unretractable curve something like the tip of a question mark. But none of this was as frightening as the noise.

The Sunday they turned on the brine in the snow-jar, there was a noise, a distant cousin, many times removed in intensity from this noise, that noise reminded Eugene Klein of the terrifying rumble of war. This noise reminded neither Nat Klein nor Rosalind Son-Lee of anything at all. There was only one word to describe this noise and that word is fear.

The wind blew for sixty-six hours in which time Rosalind and Nat rarely slept, rarely ate, and rarely spoke.

The waited.

They waited for either the seam of their Blacks of Greenock tent to snap away their lives, or the wind to stop.

The wind stopped.

It was understandably exhausted.

Nat wrote a short note to the manufacturers of the Blacks tent. The note said, "Thanks". He did not post it, there are no post boxes in the snow-jar.

The moment the wind stopped the better prepared, but no less apprehensive party on Lake Sidon shores knew they had a Thylacine. They radioed Henk Van Der Sarr. Henk Van Der Sarr was understandably delighted.

The moment the wind stopped, the water swept back to the other side of the Pool of Bethesda and set about freezing again. The pines straightened up, their DNA pondering the survival possibilities of horizontal growth. The pole of the Black's tent had no intention of ever returning to vertical and the top sixteen inches of King David's peak decided they liked it just as much down here as up there.

The moment the wind stopped Rosalind rolled over onto the lying awake body of Nat and kissed him passionately on the lips. It had taken her sixty-six hours to arrive at the decision, before the seam breaks, and they die, she is going to know what it feels like to touch a boy there. It felt remarkable warm and luscious.

The moment wind stopped Henrick Kohl and Col Stewart set out to do what they were briefed to do, capture the Thylacine. They had carefully assessed the difficulties, and the difficulties are substantial. The terrain a-top the plateaux or on its eaves is messy with lakes and ground uncertain whether to be lake or ground. The animals they presume, can travel swiftly. The weather swifter. There is no know trap or lure or decoy. There is only fear. "And what wolves fear", says Henrick Kohl, "is fire."

Fire in this case equals flares, hundreds and hundreds of flares, ringing the escarpment. A net of flares is a trap of fire, once the wolf is in its centre. There are, Henrick points out, three logical places to set the trap. The first and best between King David's peak and the Temple. The second, the adja-cent valley, between the Temple and Mount Jerusalem, the third, Jaffa Vale. A fourth, would naturally be Lake Sidon, this he dismisses, for although it is topographically adequate, it is politically insensitive. For as much as he admires the zeal Jacky and Harold have brought to their task, as Henk Van Der Sarr says, "Zeal, Henrick, is a volatile energy."

They will direct Jacky and Harold's attention to a decoy sighting, sched-uled to take place this very morning on Solomon's Jewels. An unmistakable two point five minutes of Thylacine sightings, moving a distant south, south west arc of their vision. On Solomon's Jewels there are many cameras and impenetrable scrub. It is a damn awful place to look for a Thylacine.

A-top King David's Peak, a band of flares, positioned for drama if not to snare, a band on the Temple, a band on Mount Zion. Yet there is no more than the overture, a second, third, fourth, and fifth tier will shrink the wolves into a cornered quarter acre on the banks of Bethesda. Each circle of flares primed to activate once the wolves trip the wires which stretch, escarpment to escarpment across the four possible entries to the valley, Damascus Gate, Gate of the Chain, Ephraim's Gate and Herods Gate. It is a day's work on skis, all the while sweeping binoculars across the valley floor, least the wolves already lie within the bounds of their trap. They do not. Although Rosalind Son-Lee and Nat Klein do, it is a trick of the light that neither Henrick Kohl or Col Stewart notice them.

Nat is sitting in meditation posture, he is whistling the wolf sutra. He has been whistling for two hours. The wolf sutra diverges in only one semitone from the body calming sutra, hence as Nat whistles, his body ceases sending pins and needles messages to a whistling mind. In the Blacks of Greenock tent Rosalind is trying to think of the words in either German or English to define what she feels. The words she has thought in alphabetical order are; anxious, confused, grown-up, guilty, lustful, proud, tender, and outside of the alphabetical order distracted, by the whistling, for the whistling is like a word, a moist word, a warm word, a luscious word, the word Rosalind Son-Lee is searching for, the word which describes what it was like after the wind stopped, the word she decides is "helium". While Rosalind thinks helium thoughts, Nat Klein whistles.

He whistles a wave. A whistle wave crosses the Pool of Bethesda, it beaches on a distant shore and is lost amongst the pencil-pines. Another whistle wave rises, brushing a cornice on King David's peak and entering the sky. Yet another ricochets down the U-shaped valley crossing the trip wire at Herods Gate, neither Henrick Kohl nor Col Stewart hear it. On Zion Hill, at exactly four forty-seven the wolves do, as they give chase to a kangaroo rat through dense horizontal scrub.

At five fifteen they cross the trip wires activating the first tier of flares. A trot becomes a canter, a canter a gallop, as either flank and the brush behind ignites. The wolves are swift. The wolves are fast. The wolves traverse the distance from the fifth to forth tier of flares in seventy-two seconds. The flares appear continuous.

> Red flares,
> red dusk,
> white wolves running.

At five eighteen, crossing a small pandanus, pencil-pine copse, one hundred and seventy metres from the Pool of Bethesda, in a crescendo blast of flares, the wolves vanish, into a flare guildered trap.

"This," says Nat, and Rosalind agrees, "Is very, very peculiar."
"This," says Nat, to Rosalind's discomfort, "smacks of quasi-science or kidnapping."

In the last glimmer of light, under the tullage of Nat's projection torch, they set out to investigate the copse. Sneaking across the heath, Nat cloaked in the black silk cape of the Green Avenger, Rosalind wearing the black burglar balaclava, they approach sleuthfully and cautiously low trees on a black heath. Halting at the edge Nat places his first index finger to his lips. "Shh." They "Shh." They cannot hear anything. Anything unaccountable, they can hear the exhausted wind, they can hear the dripping of snow melt from pandanus and pine, they can hear their heart beats, loud and clear, like a drum beat. Nat moves, ever so quietly, ever so expectantly, into the copse, towards the trap. Red mist hanging low in the pencil-pines, the smell of gunpowder. Flare butts in a tight semi-circle, two syringes in the heath.

There is but one question, and that is, "Who?"

They ponder, and ponder, and ponder. Rosalind concluding, "Joseph", and Nat concluding, "us".

"But how could Joseph?" Nat asks questioningly.

"But, how could we?" Rosalind asks with equal incomprehension.

The answers are intriguingly identical, "because we programmed it."

"There is a button," says Rosalind, "A button on the consul, the button marked U {the same shape as the valley} which, when pressed in the right sequence, will undo."

"Will it undo," asks Nat, "The moment twenty minutes ago when the Thylacines vanished from the snow-jar?"

"I don't know."

"Will it undo," he adds, "The moment four days ago when we climbed through the window?"

"I don't know." She whispers, as they trudge arm in arm across the ice crusted heath.

"Will it undo", he queries, fanning embers of a nervous fire, "Eugene and the woman in the fez?"

"I don't know." She shrugs, holding her hands above the sparks.

"Will it undo", he questions, as he lies in the dark nitrate night, "Whoever it is we let into the snow-jar, be they Joseph or Joseph's ghost?"

"I don't know." She mutters, barely a tongue length from his ear.

"Will it undo", he asks, finally, repentantly, "The wolf we ought perhaps to have left, alive or dead, on the real distant tiers."

"I don't know," says Rosalind, a quiver in her voice, "If we should undo the wolf."

It occurred to Nat, even then, such a manifestly useful button could not, really exist.

In the morning they will begin a search. It will be called, at one moment, the search for the wolves, at another, the search for the ghosts, if it was the ghost of Joseph who has captured the wolf. It will always however, be in secret, the search for the window.

33. Rosalind and Nat seek a Window.

They journey east, through the Gate of the Chain, towards Lake Sidon camp, for that is where the mystery will be solved. They journey tardily. Rosalind, following a precarious zigzag up the ice, is thinking about Nat, who she should never have let him near the program, all the instability which has surfaced in the model can be traced straight back to Nat. All the instability in her life can be traced straight back to Nat. Rosalind Son-Lee began to wonder if she should not undo more than the ghosts in the model. If she should not undo Nat. As soon as they are back, or perhaps, as soon as he helps her repair the model, then again maybe, as soon, she hesitates, for this really is confusing, all these new "helium" thoughts, so light and dizzy and so unscientific.

Mist in the east, clutters the valley below Mount Jerusalem escarpment cloud over King David's peak, a single puff of whiteness over the Temple, on the roof of a pine forest, they sit in the sunlight. Nat having brushed fresh snow, chipped unpliable ice from the dolomite boulder, and gallantly shared his cape. He swivels his face, perpendicular to his torso, his eyes staring up, gazing at Rosalind, who is faintly embarrassed.

"The ghosts have stolen your smile."

She smiles it back.

"The model works Nat."

"I never thought it wouldn't."

"It wasn't a mistake I could have anticipated."

"Not at all Rosalind."

"When we find the camp of the ghosts, do you think it would be possible to send a message to the past?"

"I think", grins Nat, "It would be unorthodox."

The message is very simple. The message is just four words. The message is, "Let them go free." Rosalind wrote it on the flaps of the tents of the ghosts in red girlish lipstick. The tents of the ghosts were exactly how, and exactly where, they imagined the tents of the ghosts to be. On Lake Sidon banks, five tents shaped like inverted ice-cream cones. A weather station, snow shoes , skis, exactly how it is in the old photos in Mersey camp.

They left the message, then left for the window.

Rosalind calculated the window to be no more than four kilometres away, via Zion Gate, beyond which they would camp, before the ponderous task of navigating the myriad of lakes and ridges which cover the plateaux heights. Beneath the canvas Rosalind turns to Nat.

"When we go back through the window, no one must know anything."

By no one she meant Elizabeth, by anything, she meant, what they did when the wind stopped blowing and what she repeats without the wind even whistling on the plateaux side of Zion Gate, no further than last time but just far enough.

The problem on the plateaux is distance. It just isn't possible to know how far you have walked when every hundred metres duplicates itself in another lake, another ridge, another bank of crusted snow. That alone would be problem enough without the mist. In the morning the mist is here, there and everywhere. It is in the vestibule of the Blacks of Greenock tent. It is escaping from every breath from mist generating lungs, it is hovering about the inside pole which bends like the tip of a question mark.

"The mist" Nat suggests, when they awake, "may not be exclusively an inside mist."

It is not. It is an inside, outside mist, which outside is the most misty mist they ever have seen. Outside is not even an outside, but a single enveloping mystery. They sit in the tent, waiting for the mist to lift, it lifts in the vestibule, it clears from around the pondering pole, but this only adds to the proportion of mist outside. Rosalind sits up in her sleeping bag and begins her journal, writing in German, writing about Nat. While Nat opens his pencil case and withdraws cobalt blue, in the express train of the imagination.

The Green Avenger and Nadia still locked in deadly intrigue with the Seventh Samurai. The first line he draws is the line of the cape, the black linen Cape he wears, he draws it very quickly in a stylized version, and follows in black, the dark bob of Nadia's hair.

Rosalind asks, "Are you drawing us?"

"No, us", he explains, " us would mean a red spectacle frame on-top Nadia's nose, and a slighter more oriental nose to boot. Us would necessitate a rucksack on the back of the Green Avenger and a snow-jar window, instead of the Vienna Express. "That", he explains, "Is us."

"Draw the moment we saw the wolves Nat."

When he does she says, "No, the wolves were closer, they were so, so close, you must remember Nat."

He drew them closer. He drew them with seven stripes rather than the eight he thought they had, and he coloured the stripes ochre rather than tan.

"Draw the camp of ghosts Nat."

They agreed on the number of tents in the camp of ghosts, but not what was in each.

"Draw the moment the wind began to blow."

"And draw", she whispered, "The moment it stopped."

He drew what she asks, and the first day of mist passes. There is nothing left to draw in the second. Sometime in the second day Nat and Rosalind agreed, they will have to do something. Something heroic. Rosalind opens the vast multi-coloured map, she spreads it out across the sleeping bags and with her small compass began to plot a course from where they thought they might be to where they thought they ought to be. She plots a perfect course, a straight line between two dots, but it doesn't fill Nat and it doesn't fill Rosalind with any joy.

They would walk for three and one quarter hours at just one kilometre an hour, a cruelly slow pace. They would walk east, south east, one hundred and one degrees, and they would start in one hours' time. They could have used a sling. A number four climbing rope, Nat mentions as the exit their orange Black's tent. A number four climbing rope might keep them together, Rosalind slung to Nat, Nat slung to Rosalind. Without the rope Nat must step into Rosalind's footprints, like a single gawky quadruped joined at the thigh. In three hours, fifteen minutes of walking, they pass no trees, they encounter no ridges, or fall into the belly of any partially frozen lakes. In three hours, fifteen, Nat Klein saw nothing but the rising of Rosalind's left foot, right foot, left foot, and Rosalind saw nothing at all. When they crawled back into their Blacks of Greenock tent they knew only that they had exchanged dots. Rosalind doesn't write anything in her journals, even the word, hopeless, doesn't seem quite hopeless enough.

Rosalind Son-Lee twists her left hand around her right index finger as Nat doodles. Nat draws a window, when he finishes his window he draws another, then another, for each time he remembers a little more, then a little more, the details of the window through which they came. It was square, or just off square. It was joined to the frame, but not to the dome with thirty-eight rivets. It was made of double glass. Drawn in proportion on three by four inch wax-paper, it comprised of an image two inches by one and fifteen sixteenths.

"It's good", says Rosalind, "but it is not big enough."

Nat takes his flashlight, placed it behind the window slide. He asks Rosalind for her spectacles, and places them in front. In the mist two point seven metres form the tent flap, he projects the familiar snow-jar window.

"All I need is one hour and one spectacle lens."

One hour later, at six twenty-five p.m. on Sunday September the fifth, an eye patched Rosalind Son-Lee climbs back through Nat's projection to land with a thump on the observation floor.

33. Bump!

Rosalind Son-Lee sits up. Nat Klein sits up. Rosalind Son-Lee dusts herself off. Nat Klein dusts himself off. Rosalind Son-Lee asks Nat Klein what Nat Klein was about to ask Rosalind Son-Lee.

"Where is the music coming from?"

The music is a drumbeat, a drumbeat joined by a flute. The music is unexpectedly familiar. The music, when played, rather than whistled is unexpectedly melodic. The music is the wolf sutra. Nat says to Rosalind what Rosalind was about to say to Nat.

"We may as well take a look."

What they saw surprises them. Not the tents even though there are five more than when they entered the snow-jar, nor the fires, they seemed perfectly compatible, given the tents. What surprises them are the lanterns, slung as they are like in the movies of old China-town. and the figures, or are they masks, for some are undoubtedly faces, with peaks, and some with eyes and one at least a gullet. They are large, standing on poles in the manner of lackadaisical herons. All bar one, which stands in the centre of Mersey camp on four canine feet. It is somebody's notion of a wolf. It is a wolf worthy of the society which surrounds it, drunken eyed, snap trapped jawed, strong, ferocious and untrue.

Nat approaches the camp, Rosalind following three steps behind. Both drumbeat and flute cease as the society notices the diminutive black capped figure, and even more diminutive eye-patched companion.

"Dr Seon!!"

"And Foo-Lee!"

The whistler of sutras, companion of wolves, at one with the ice, the wind, the mountains, the enigmatic hero. They'd followed his exploits, the great trek upon ice, over the plateaux and down through the vales, the great battle with wind, with ice mist and snow, but Dr Seon is taller and older than he, who walks out of the snow jar in his black silk cape.

"Huh!" they whisper.

"Who does he think he is?" they whisper.

"Who does she think she is?" they whisper.

Di Jacobsen stands feet firm before the entrance to Mersey camp. She says, "Huh" the loudest. Repeating it loudest, paradoxically the moment she recognizes Nat Klein and Rosalind Son-Lee.

The recognition embarrasses her, the recognition causes her to flinch for one dangerous moment. She walks towards them, to steer them away from a profound misunderstanding, or to steer a profound understanding away from the only society to have ever voted her President. She steers them into a Black Cab taxi whose destination is Shelley Street, Elsternwick. Their arrival given ten minutes notice by a brief and malevolent phone call.

The I-Ching had for once forewarned Mary O'Becket. She acted very quickly, she acted very calmly, and she hoped very prudently.

She ran a bath. They would be tired, they would be sweaty. She warmed on the oil heater the clothes she had found for Nat and those she had found for Rosalind. She asked Eugene to order pizzas at Don Giovanni's Pizza Palace. It was Sunday night, one of Eugene's three nights, for the I-Ching had wisely counselled Mary, given their age, and the fact that she was about to leave for Helsinki, to curfew this relationship to Sunday, Tuesday, and Friday. She rang Dr Son-Lee. They had spoken before, it is the call she'd promised him and is now glad to deliver. She rang Paul. She drank one very large whisky and opened the door of her flat.

Rosalind Son-Lee lay in the bath with her one eye patched and her other eye lensed. Mary O'Becket showed her the clothes she'd had fun finding in the St. Vincent de Paul. They are slightly silver and slightly eastern rather than the drab, timid, school-girlish look Rosalind would choose for herself.

"It was just an idea, you don't have to wear them."

Rosalind smiled the smile Mary expected. And wore them to Nat's bewilderment, looking, exotic, wonderful, beautiful.

"What was it like, in the snow-jar?"

"Cold."

She asks Nat the same question, he answers, "Icy".

They ate pizza around Mary's coffee table. It was not a relaxed pizza. Not everyone was glad to see everyone. Nat wasn't happy to see Eugene in Marys flat. Dr Son-Lee wasn't happy to see Nat. Rosalind Son-Lee was very nervous about seeing her father. Eugene was very nervous about seeing Nat. Paul was nervous about seeing Nat.

Genevieve wouldn't come in.

PART 6.

Proceedings From The Society

of the Wolf

Hobart Mercury January 1982
No Dams!

The "No Dams!" campaign against the Gordon below Franklin dam appears to have spread from the Apple Isle to the national stage. "No Dam Greenies" have taken their protests to the national capital in a sign of heightened tension around the planned, and approved, Gordon below Franklin Dam.

A spokesperson for the Hydro Electricity Commission, stated while the H.E.C. is a good corporate citizen who believes in the rule of law, and the sanctity of process, you cannot say the same thing of their opposition. The dam is both essential to the future well-being of Tasmania and has been approved by the Tasmanian Parliament. It is, he noted, a Tasmanian dam, not a Canberra dam, and the Tasmanian people have spoken.

34. In which Eugene has a Dream.

Eugene Klein knew when he woke, he'd been somewhere inexplicable. It was raining where he'd been. It is raining where he wakes. A soft rain here. A rain, which made a noise, when it fell as rain, like rice grains tumbling, and when it fell as snow, there, no noise at all. The houses in his dream were grey slate with steep pitched roofs, the trees predominantly fir, more trees than houses, at least on Eugene side of the express train. The express was travelling south, or so Eugene thought as he entered the dream, before he noticed the first houses, the first fir trees, the first snow, and realized in what hemisphere he was travelling. The express train was travelling north, away from the sun. A dull sun obscured by cloud, so low, the express train periodically pierces it.

Eugene had ordered coffee. He believes he has ordered coffee, he accepts there is a reason he is waiting, he accepts there is a reason he is travelling, and he hopes later in the dream that reason will be fathomable.

It will be, and very soon. It will be fathomable in the dream, but inexplicable when he wakes.

The reason is simple.

Nadia is on this train.

At first Eugene doesn't recognize her. She is standing beside an oriental in a black silk cape at the other end of the dining car. She is wearing stiletto heeled shoes and a decidedly vampish dress and arguing with the oriental gentleman in a language Eugene doesn't understand. He does not need to understand, to know, Nadia does not wish any longer to be the oriental's accomplice.

In the final reel of Eugene Klein's dream, he notices Nadia and Nadia notices him.

It is raining on the roof of Marys Elsternwick flat. It is very, very, early in the morning. A half-moon sets over Hudson's Bay. He can watch without moving, without stirring Mary, the squally September clouds, moonlight on wave-tops, freighters in the channel.

Nadia Kaminski is dead. She died in central Europe sometime between August nineteen forty-four and August nineteen forty-five, between the ages of twenty-six and twenty-seven. She was so young. They were so young.

Did she die on this train?

Did the oriental, with whom she is arguing murder her?

Is this why he is dreaming it?

Eugene Klein had flown, forty-seven sorties over Europe. He has bombed the Frankfurt, Stuttgart rail line at Mannheim, the Munich, Salzburg line at Rosenheim, the Hamburg, Berlin line at Wittenberg, and the Mannheim, Strasburg line at Griesheim, he is knowledgeable of the rail system of Greater Germany. Of those he has bombed, he knows only the Munich, Salzburg line climbs sufficiently to pass forests of spruce and fir. Nadia is not travelling the Munich, Salzburg line, if she was, she would be travelling east or west.

In the half moon light, on the only findable scrap of paper, an international aerogram addressed to Zoey in Helsinki, Eugene Klein began to map all he could remember of his dining carriage journey. It will not be an easy matter, but it will not be impossible, to superimpose enough information on a detailed atlas of Europe and find her.

Mary O'Becket brought two aerograms on her way to the Museum. One to replace that, addressed to Zoey, on which Eugene has begun his map and one on which he can continue. A map begun is a journey begun, a journey begun on aerograms, should, she laughed, when he'd apologized, naturally proceed on aerograms, underneath the magical words, "Par Avion" especially the journey of an airman.

"The journey I dreamt was on an express train."

Did that dissuade her, not for a moment, for Mary loves trains, she loves them nearly as much as Thomas Wolf did. Especially trains in distant, wonderful countries with Sanskrit script on the tickets and third-class carriages full of colour.

No one, Mary has ever known, has mapped a dream. She imagined the wondrous landscapes, the mysterious places within her own dreams, and she wondered how Eugene might fix on paper the turbulent uncertainty of the sleeping world she knows, then she thought of the multi-coloured map and grins.

She brought an extra two aerograms. He will need them.

On the St. Kilda road tram, she composes the main points of her letter to Zoey. "The man Gene, the one in the last letter, and yes, the letter before that, is unexpectedly interesting, unexpectedly warm, unexpectedly knowing and unexpectedly unexpected."

She must think of a way to tell Zoey of the map of dreams, she could of course send the original, given that it is drawn on an aerogram addressed to Zoey in Helsinki, but won't. "The savings are on track, it won't be long now, although the interest in the T-shirts she suspects has peaked, for without the wolves it is unsustainable. Where are the wolves? You won't believe this Zoey, someone has hijacked them from the snow-jar. Isn't that just weird?"

35. What is Henk Van Der Sarr up To?

Jacky Lambert has pondered the tent flap message, "Let them go free!" for two mind rattled days. Only one thing is certain, it refers to the wolves.

"I have no reason to believe," Jacky cautions Jacky, "that the wolves are anything but free, yet I have no facts at all."

In the absence of facts Jacky Lambert is uncomfortable. An uncomfortable Jacky asks ten questions originally only to herself.

The ten questions are:

"If one of us four did not write the message, who did?"

"If the wolves were not, as they patently weren't on Solomon's Jewels, where were they?"

"Why did they not further investigate the only certain sighting at Jaffa Vale?"

"If the agenda of this party is to photograph the wolves, why have only she and Harold been involved in photography?"

"What motivation has Henk Van Der Sarr for finding the wolves?"

"Where is Col Stewart?"

"Where is Henrick Kohl?"

"What was stored in the two locked bags laying under the trip-wire spools in Henrick's private store tent?"

"Why is Harold Nicholson not equally curious about the things which do not tally in this camp?"

"Is this what Rosalind Son-Lee may describe as Agatha Christie science?"

She tells Harold, who is about to begin for the third, which is usually but not always his final time, unpacking and repacking his rucksack, that this morning she thought it may be illuminating to visit Jaffa Vale and not the Jewels.

Harold says, "Damn, damn, and double damn, I've packed the wrong spare guernsey."

Harold repacks. Jacky bides her time, counting the insects imbedded in the snow, on which currawongs graze. How many insects per square metre, how many currawongs per square kilometre, what chance a wolf preying upon a currawong. The model, Rosalind's model did not program this peculiar source of nibbling, she must tell Rosalind to amend this, if Rosalind is still interested in the wolf.

Climbing Jaffa Vale on a blustery, blustery morn, the wind venturi's through the gate, pushing, and pushing, and pushing against them, but easing as they drop into the pines where they found the first photo of the wolf.

In Jaffa Vale in fickle spring sunlight, parting and passing scurrying clouds, Jacky Lambert asks her final two questions to the wind.

"Where have all the cameras gone?"

"What the heck is Henk Van Der Sarr up to?"

Henk Van Der Sarr summarizes the situation viz-a-viz Mersey camp succinctly and accurately in five words, "Gentlemen, welcome to the circus."

Sir Richard Clover says, "Here, here," from the seat to the left of the podium, and the management committee of the Museum of Victoria nod their agreement.

"Order," Henk Van Der Sarr commences with a word they all understand, "Order is what a Museum represents, the evolution of the species, Genus-Order-Species, the evolution of man, the Neanderthal man, the birth of civilization, the classic age of order, the dark age of irrationality, for yes, amongst men, chaos can be victorious over order. It is time gentlemen that order attacked."

His strategy is simple.

His strategy is elegant.

His strategy has proven successful in the past. His strategy is illustrative of the ingenuity of man, what Henk Van Der Sarr proposes is damming Mersey camp. He means, of course, the Mersey Camp in Gallery Five, the Mersey Camp around the snow jay, he and the Hydro Electricity Commission has long ago dammed the real Mersey River valley.

He has drawn illustrations, of his proposal, wonderful colour illustrations of the South West wing of the Victorian Museum where the rivers flowing from the snow jar Tiers and gathered into a small pondage to drive, as he says, "the turbines of progress." He has drawn the Mersey Camp turbines in cross section to illustrate the wonder which hydroelectricity is. Nature in perfect synchrony with man.

"The snow-jar," He emphasises, "Barring the odd road here, an occasional aqueduct there, a diversion somewhere around here and a spillway or two will, at all times, retain its wilderness character, as," he smiles, "As the original."

36. The Pageant of the Wolf.

In Mersey Camp, the Society of the Wolf performs twice a day, what Henk Van Der Sarr refers to as, "the circus."

It is not a circus.

It is a pageant.

It is also both surprisingly professional and surprisingly popular.

Henk Van Der Sarr would not concede that. He has no interest in conceding that, only in having it stopped. Henk Van Der Sarr would like it stopped, not because it is popular, but because it is a loose end. Henk Van Der Sarr does not like loose ends, "They have the habit of unravelling the best laid plans."

The pageant begins in the dream-time of the wolf, narrated by the black capped figure of Dr Seon performed by Di Jacobson.

"In the first great ice age of the world," the narration begins, "The wolf alpina parted from its lowland Thylacine cousins, paler in colour, broader in paw, brushier tailed, it hunted an ice bound world. Preying upon the walla-bies, the bush tailed possum and the Tasmanian cat," and onwards through Rosalind Son-Lee's model. Migrating egrets, airborne puppets on long cane handles soar above the narrator, unwary bandicoots, miniscule antechinus parade before her feet. The clarinets commence the tune, the sutra of the wolf begins, from afar a drum beat tapping as the wolf creeps from the mist. The wolf puppet brays and snarls his way passed fearful children, who gape and screech as egrets fly and bandicoots dash for cover.

As centuries pass, the ice contracts, melting back into the craggy rocks and high and windy ridges. Following the ice, the wolves, retreating into the ridgeland landscape which we behold inside the snow-jar. The audience follow the wolf and the birds up the path which leads inside the Observation Hide. There Di Jacobson as Dr Seon sits in meditation posture, whistling the wolf into view. Her whistling is joined by the clarinet, joined by the flute and piccolo, which in the confines of the hide create a haunting, distant air.

It does not however attract the wolf.

It didn't attract the wolf yesterday, or the day before. In the absence of wolves the audiences are beginning to dwindle. In the absence of audiences Henk Van Der Sarr decides it is time to begin dismantling, "the circus".

Four members of the Museum maintenance staff flanked by Museum security begin dismantling the Mersey Camp foyer. They remove Joseph Klein's eyeglasses, Joseph Klein's sextant and Joseph Klein's statue complete with cocky hat. They remove the glass cased wallaby, bush tailed possum and Tasmanian cat to return them to mammalia. They unhook the photographs, unscrew the Perspex covers and carefully roll the maps into long cardboard cylinders. They dismantle the white zigzagging display screens and remove the sign "Magic, Myth or Monster?" replacing it with another, "Exhibit tem-porally closed".

The Society of the Wolf watch in disbelief from four fifteen to five twen-ty-five when the Museum staff finish their labours for the day. The Society of the Wolf, then enter in mass into the foyer, as the Museum staff slam the exit. They are understandable perplexed. They mill about wondering, "what is to be done?"

"Is it time to scurry or time to defend?" A question which splits the Society neatly into thirds.

"Defence," reasoned the first of the thirds, "Being out of the question since we are undeniably trespassing."

"On public land," quibbled the second third, "Providing public entertainment for the public benefit."

"And what," asks Jacky Wang, representing the don't knows, the largest third by far "Of the wolf?"

"The wolf," answers Di Jacobsen president of all, "Is our sole concern, it is fundamental, it goes without saying." And so, it must for she doesn't mention it again; she mentioned the Society, its short, gallant history, she mentioned herself, but only in passing, although she passed that way four times. She calls for a show of hands. The Society of the wolf showed its hands. The don't knows won. It passes this evening as a kind of decision.

The workmen began at eight thirty sharp, lighting a camp stove in the corner of the foyer, boiling their morning cuppa.

The press arrived late, at eight fifty-seven confused by the message left on his answering machine. The message said, "Welcome to the first day of the war between the packs."

Stan "Scoop" Munro stood in the centre of the foyer and photographs the Museum staff dismantling the partitions up to the first flimsy barricade of the Society of the Wolf, a barricade of puppets. He photographed the Society members, he photographed the barricades, and he photographed the Museum staff but none of these photographs were particularly newsworthy, because at that moment the war between the packs was a very polite war indeed, not a war to sell newspapers, not that sort of war at all.

He'd wasted an hour, snapped a complete roll of thirty-six shots. He'd interviewed Di Jacobson. He would have liked to interview Henk Van Der Sarr, but Henk van Der Sarr was as usual indisposed. He would have liked to ask Henk van der Sarr, what the heck he is up to?

In the absence of Henk Van Der Sarr he returned to his office with neither he thought, a good story nor a good photograph. He was right about the story. Wrong about the photograph. He'd photographed Sara Miles, the most photogenic of the society members, standing before Darky Seymour holding a threatening jerry-bar in hand. The image was war-like, it was, everyone in the office agreed, a good snap. It was not however one hundred percent accurate, being more a trick of perspective than an act of violence.

A wonderful photo, but a dud of a story.

The photo, not the story, made the afternoon edition.

The afternoon edition arrived on Flinders Street at three fifteen. It arrived on Swanson Street at three twenty-one, the corner of Swanson and Latrobe at three twenty-three. A copy reached the Museum library at three twenty-seven, the management board room at three forty-six, the shop steward of the Miscellaneous Workers Union, Museum of Victoria Branch at three fifty-seven, the barricade of the Society of the Wolf at four exactly. The afternoon edition reached Camberwell at four-o-one, Elwood at four-o-nine. Genevieve did not buy the *Herald*, it isn't her kind of paper. Mary did. A small parcel of *Melbourne Heralds* arrived five-o-one at Hobart airport, five twenty-six Hobart central and five twenty-nine at the Hobart offices of the H.E.C. Henk Van Der Sarr, took seven words to sum up the situation, "Every photo is worth a thousand lies."

37. Doing and Undoings.

By the time the afternoon edition of the *Melbourne Herald* reached Henk Van Der Sarr, Nat Klein and Rosalind Son-Lee had entered via the fire escape, the south west wing, to press if it is not too late the button on the main frame computer marked U.

At five fifty-seven on Tuesday September seven Rosalind Son-Lee pressed the button marked U.

Nothing happened.

It did not undo the moment they entered the snow-jar.

It did not undo the sighting of the wolf, which both Rosalind and Nat hoped it would not.

It did not undo the moment when the wind began or the moment when the wind ceased exhausted, and Rosalind is relieved it does not.

It did not undo the evening of the flares which both Rosalind and Nat had hoped that it would.

And it did not undo the camp bed in the cartoon room where on Monday, Wednesday, Thursday, and Saturday, Eugene Klein calls his home, as Nat had wished, so much, that it might.

However, it is not true that the button marked U, undid nothing at all.

At six eleven the undoing, undid a noise, a noise which sounds at once like both a cracking and a splitting, a noise which began in the snow-jar, under the ice, deep in the permasnow, deep as the poly-pipes, as deep as the programme. The temperature on the monitors rose eleven degrees in eleven minutes and across the centre of lake Sidon an ice crack, creaks.

Di Jacobsen said, "It is an omen."

It is undoubtedly an omen.

And it undid, Nat discovers later, as he sits in his airman's seat, wearing his leather flying cap and goggles with his pencils spread across his desk, the story, and cartoon, "The New Adventures of the Green Avenger." Against Nat's will Nadia walks away, out of the frame, out of the set, proud and deviant away from the confrontation between the Green Avenger and the Seventh Samurai towards one lone character at the distant end of the dining car.

And now, whenever Nat draws the cape he draws himself within it, how it was in that distant land in the snow-jar with Rosalind. Thoughts of Rosalind interrupt his waking, his walking, his sleeping, his talking. They do not interrupt his dreaming. They are his dreaming. If he drew a cartoon of his dreaming, it would only be a cartoon. If he drew her face as it was in the snow, timidly smiling behind the balaclava, it would be no more than a drawing. He could not wipe snow from her eyelashes without smudging them, for that is what is wrong with cartoons, they are only dreams on paper, you cannot touch them, and you cannot kiss them.

Eugene Klein yearned to touch, yearned to kiss, the drawing in his dream, half a dining car away and moving tentatively towards him, one, two, three, stiletto steps. They pass a siding, dense forests either side, a branch line and a small five to ten dwelling hamlets to the right.

Nadia is five steps away. For the first time since she began to walk, for the first time in forty years she smiles the nervous, incomparable smile of a sparkler.

She speaks, "Gene?"

There are many things Eugene wishes to ask, to know about the events in her life since their lives parted. About whether she ever thinks of him how he thinks of her, or whether she has seen his model of the wolf. "My wolf, remember the wolf Nadia?" He asks none of these, all he can say as he stands inches from his dream is, "Nadia, I'm beginning to be old."

"You're sweating," Mary whispers, "Why are you sweating."

It is Tuesday, he is with Mary, Mary who is wearing only the T-shirt she has silk screened this evening, a photograph from the *Herald*, the photo of Darky Seymour attacking the girl, with the words "No Dams!" scrawled across it. He always dreams of Nadia when he is with Mary, Why?

"I was dreaming," Paul says, blinking between there and now, "of the express train."

"I know where it is." whispers Mary.

"How?"

"I threw the I-Ching. It is going home, it is heading to Zakopane, and I think your father is on it."

Eugene has up till now, barring his sleeping arrangements, managed to ignore the I-Ching, regarding it as something pseudo-scientific, like E.S.P and therefore mumbo-jumbo. And although Eugene doesn't know how many kilometres of rail cross the Reich land, except it is a large number. And although he knows the express train could just as likely be travelling anywhere on this system.

He also knows, it isn't, the moment Mary told him, Eugene knew, she is absolutely right.

"Mary", whispers Paul, "I'm beginning to be old."

"Old men," Mary returned the whisper, "don't invent snow-jars."

38. A crack cracks.

Even before the helicopter beat, chuu-chuu, chuu-chuu, chuu-chuu, chopper, over Zion Gate descending into the vale towards lake Siddon camp. The snow had begun to melt, the frost begun to thaw, the winter begun to bate, as up in the escarpment and all-around white turns grey, grey-green, green.

Even before the helicopter beat; chuu-chuu, chuu-chuu, chuu-chuu, chopper, above the five expedition tents shaped like inverted ice-cream cones and with the words, "Let them go free" written on each flap. The ground beneath the pines had cleared of snow, as had the crags but not the gullies in which deeply crusted banks of snow reminiscent of a glacial past lay melting.

Even before the helicopter beat; chuu-chuu, chuu-chuu, chuu-chuu, chopper, over Lake Sidon, puddles of water had begun thawing and freezing, day and night and day and night and each day a little bigger and each night freezing with a little less conviction. But only once the helicopter descended towards the ice did the ice finally crack.

The helicopter landed ten metres away from Jacky Lambert, who'd been peering through her binoculars ever since she'd first heard the noise; chuu-chuu, chuu-chuu, chuu-chuu, chopper, peering and wondering, "What the heck?" The pilot steps out of his chopper, removes a fibreglass helmet and says, "Whoo!"

He says, "I wouldn't skate on that lake lady."

He is tall and lean and tanned and blonde. He didn't shave today, he didn't shave yesterday, but he may have shaved the day before that. He wears riding boots, moleskin trousers, and ought to be wearing the "Akubra" hat tucked behind the seat of his chopper but isn't, on account of the wind.

He says, "Lady you're requested to accompany me back to Hobart, you and a joker called Harold Nicholson."

Jacky asked the aviator , what he saw flying in.

"Lakes Lady, the lands lousy with lakes."

"No tracks, no animals?"

"That I did Lady."

"Call me Jacky."

"Yes Lady."

He saw wallabies on the heath near Tullah Lagoon. He saw thousands upon thousands of thawing lakes, thawing ridges thawing streams. He saw north to south, east to west from Mersey Crag to Great Pine Tier, the Wailing Wall to New Year's Lake, and everything he saw was melting. He saw more than Nat Klein and Rosalind Son-Lee saw in seven days of journey. More than Eugene Klein and Martin McKenzie had ever imagined as they built the shell and landscaped the floor of the snow-jar and more than either Joseph Klein or Arlo Levi had seen in seven expeditions and seventeen months, but he did not see a Thylacine.

A half hour latter Jacky points out of the chopper cockpit into the relief map of a thawing Tiers the place where Joseph first saw the Thylacine.

"Imagine what he would have given to hover five thousand feet above the peak of Mount Jerusalem."

"You can imagine," yells Jacky, " how it must have been in the last great Ice Age."

"You can imagine," Jacky yells above the chopper cabin noise, "how a man who'd seen the wild wolves of Europe would be filled with nostalgia by this sight."

"But you cannot imagine," Jacky concludes, "what he thought, what he felt, to tread untrodden ground."

Into the untrodden ground of a brand-new age, Anita Craige guided tours, every hour, on the hour, into Henk Van Der Sarrs vision of the Tiers. A Tiers where man and nature are in unison, constructed in the foyer of Mersey Camp all that morning by the sub-committee in charge of exhibitions {in view of a general union ban}. Mary O'Becket joined the second tour wearing her "No Dams!" T-shirt. She looked at the photographs. They are of water, spillways, aqueducts, streams and lakes. There are photographs of snow and photographs of rain, photographs of turbines and a map of the Tiers which is both familiar and bizarre. There are lakes where lakes hadn't been before and streams where streams hadn't sprouted. Mary O'Becket, alone amongst the party looked at the photos, studied the maps and asked Anita Crag sensible questions. The lady with the pink parasol strode directly to the barricades, waved a pink wave in the Mersey Camp direction and demanded to know why, "You bludgers haven't got a job to go to?" While the man in the cashmere cardigan passed five dollars over, by way, he explained, of donation, and asked Mary O'Becket, "Where on earth did you buy that T-shirt?"

He became her fist sale in the second spring of T-shirt sales.

Mary O'Becket hoped for a glorious second spring of T-shirt sales, a long second spring and a bright second spring. She hoped that hope for five long minutes before she heard the crack. The crack which Nat and Rosalind had undone, that crack which finally cracked.

Boy. oh boy, did the crack, crack. The crack, cracked the entire length of the snow-jar lake, it cracked the fraction which is supposed to be water and the fraction which is supposed to be glass, it cracked the snow and cracked the ridges and cracked the black poly-pipe outflow and its mini solenoid valve. And that was the crack which started the flood.

The flood swirled through the pencil-pine and pandanus grove, uprooting pandanus, uprooting pine, gushing and gurgling downstream to the camp. Lapping the barricades, swamping the tents, such that the tent which housed the relief map, and the tent which housed Susan Wong and the tent which housed the President floated like Monet water-lilies on Mersey Camp pond.

No one in the Society of the Wolf dared ask the President if this were another omen.

Mary O'Becket longed to dash up the fire escape steps, to tell Eugene, show Eugene, ask Eugene, if it were an omen. But today is Wednesday and Wednesday isn't Eugene day, so sent she a Society of the Wolf postcard on which she wrote.

Genesis 8, 17-18, And the flood was forty days upon the earth; and the waters increased, and bare up the ark, and it was lift up upon the earth. And the waters prevailed and were increased greatly upon the earth.

She posted it immediately.

39. Night and Day.

Eugene Klein briefly read the postcard.

He then clipped it to a three by three metre display board painted white. He clipped it to an alligator clip in the top right-hand corner, the corner which approximates today. There are two display boards, one white, one black, the black with a white moon painted in its top left corner, the white with a black sun. The postcard from Mary he clipped fifteen centimetres to the right and slightly below this sun. The two display boards are not a map, but they are a landscape, the landscape of night and the landscape of day. One alone would not solve the puzzle of the dream, one alone would not find Nadia.

The white display board begins March six, nineteen-o-eight it begins in Lake Zakopane, where Joseph wrote in childish hand.

Dear Mummy,

It snowed last night. The snow was blue. Yesterday I heard a wolf howl. Do wolves kill you mummy? Daddy says they do. Tomorrow I'm going to see the wolf. Daddy says I will.

Love Joseph.

It finished with Mary's postcard.

40. Project Romulus.

Henk Van Der Sarr met a showered and fresh Jacky and Harold in the foyer of his Salamanca Place office. He apologizes for the abruptness in which he has gathered them to discuss, "The future; yours, mine, ours."

"The Tiers," he asks, "Is it not a unique asset, a unique responsibility."

He places a fatherly arm around each of their shoulders as he walks them along the corridor to briefing room five, looking solemnly ahead he asks, "Help me in this humbling responsibility." Henk Van Der Sarr cannot pronounce the letters "th" or the word "humbling".

He leads them through the doors of conference room five to behold his humble vision.

"Project...Romulus."

Project Romulus is a building, misnamed the "camp". It is a building which will rise step-wise from Lake Salome shores as four prefabricated triangular wedges, appearing from a distant bank as four tents on a hillside each emerging from the apex of the tent below, a vision duplicating Nat Klein pagoda extension in his very private book of inventions. Side on the building resembles four tents piggy-backing and from above a giant basking reptile. It can be added to both vertically and horizontally, it is self-contained, non-polluting, and aesthetically complementary to the jaw-edge escarpment ridges. "Project Romulus" is also three Perspex enclosed observation walks, the first curving eastward to the Pool of Siloam, the second departing the first and curving southwards onto the heath, and the third rising dramatically, north, north west above the camp, onto the ice of Mount Ophel. Each observation walk will terminate in a perplex observation dome, which given the nature of the weather on the Tiers, "he need not elaborate," will be complete with television consuls, broadcasting both life of the Tiers and recreated images.

The "Camp" Jacky notes, has the unsettling, albeit luxuriant air of a ski lodge.

However, it is not the camp which interests Jacky, nor the maps, nor the photographs, nor the one to one hundred scale replicas of "Project Romulus" complete with a heliport. She smiles her most gracious smile and proceeds to ask the questions she has waited four days to ask.

"What happened to the photographs of the wolf?"

He is glad she asked, very glad she asked. "The original has been sent to Europe, to be, in the vernacular, fingerprinted. A number of copies have been marvellously reproduced and displayed here in briefing room five. A wall mounted version in which the animal has been highlighted, its outlines clarified, its stripes etched in, a postcard version of the original ghostly outline. Here, you must have some."

"Why were the cameras removed from Jaffa Vale?"

"An over-diligent Henrick Kohl, I'm afraid. I asked only that he personally check each, he understood that he ought to return them, they are here, by all means return them to the Tiers, and naturally do not hesitate to ask for anything else, our considerable recourses are at your call."

"Why was the Jaffa Vale sighting not fully explored?"

"A tactical decision, perhaps not the right decision but Henrick is not a biologist."

"Perhaps," Jacky suggests, "the biologists ought to have been consulted."

"Naturally, you shall be in the future."

"And what has become of Her Kohl?"

"Dear Henrick, has been called on a mission."

She did not ask of Henrick's mission. She should have. Unlikely though that Henk Van Der Sarr would think it politic her knowing. At that very moment, in view of briefing room five, on the key-side three of Salamanca Place Henrick unloads from grey lorry to grey steamer the container caging two living Thylacines.

The steamer, *Henry the Navigator* Singapore bound, beginning leg one of a journey, described in the pamphlet printed in twelve European languages under the title, "The Myth Materializes", as a Tour de Force of European capitals. Inside the container the temperature kept a crisp six degrees celsius via a system of solar heat exchanges designed specifically for the H.E.C. by Martin McKenzie.

The steamer, *Henry the Navigator* will sail this evening, it will sail direct, it will carry a cargo of Tasmanian salmon and apples which the Thylacines will develop a gluttonous appetite for, shunning frozen antechinus and Deloraine hare.

In Singapore they will board a Lufthansa flight for Dusseldorf, where on October the twenty sixth there will be no necessity for Martin McKenzie's inventiveness. In Dusseldorf on October the twenty sixth it will be identical in every measurable climatic variable to point four of a degree and three kilometres an hour wind chill, to the afternoon of September the ninth in the snow-jar, except in the snow-jar it was raining.

A rain which tumbles from bilious clouds, ponding the puddles and torrenting the streams, squelching the heath and turning snow into gelatine and ice into snow. A rain which rains with a daring intensity and a breathtaking abandon. In the second hour of the rain the lake, which the flood had formed and had begun to subside in Mersey Camp, rose again two inches, in the third and fourth hour it crept a further inch lapping the campaign cot of Di Jacobson's high ground tent.

41. Day and Night.

"Is it us who fail our dreams, or our dreams which demand too much of us?" Eugene isn't looking at Mary, possibly he isn't even asking her. He is looking at the rain. The rain is still falling. The monitors have measured one hundred and fifteen millimetres, it is seven degrees celsius and still, the rain falling vertically.

Marys answer, had she been asked, would have been, "It is us, it is always us."

She wasn't asked.

Only when he sleeps with Mary does Eugene Klein dream the dream. The dream does not always begin where the last dream ended, for time is of another dimension on the black side of the display board. The dream he dreamt this night begins as he enters the dining car, ushered by a waiter in a black dress suit to sit at the table at the distant end from Nadia.

"Why can't I," asks Eugene, "sit where I shall be closer?"

But no, answers the waiter adopting a tone more authoritive than his uniform, "It is only for you to wait." To wait, such an insufferable occupation, to be told to wait by a man in a black dress suit an added unpleasantness. His only consolation, knowing the immediate future. He asks, if he may order coffee, and it appears he may order anything at all, although the waiter felt unobliged to explain if anything ordered might ever be served.

Eugene Klein sat. Eugene Klein watched. Eugene Klein timed, assuming an average speed of eighty kilometres per hour, the distance in seconds between sidings, boom gates and bridges, any detail which may betray to a navigator, this rail lines presence, this rail lines destination.

Thirteen kilometres, two bridges, one four-kilometre siding, a small grey slate township, from the moment he sat, until the moment Nadia entered the carriage. The moment Nadia entered the dream repeated. The rain which fell as rain and the rain which fell as snow, at exactly the same moment, in exactly the same intensity. He passed the same siding, the same signal. And has the same inexplicable feeling as he wakes, as he always wakes after the dream, to scribble on Marys aerograms, two bridges and a siding in the land, which each dream confirms, is indeed what the I-Ching predicted, somewhere in the Tatra mountains travelling towards Zakopane.

42. In which we learn of the Existence of Invention 29B.

When Henk Van Der Sarr saw the waters rising, the tents floating like water-lilies on a pea-green pond, the pencil-pines bumping, boom po-pop-boom, boom po-pop-boom against the tangle of puppetry and hope which are the barricades, he re-ordered his strategy, moved forward by a month. He would open his recruitment tent today. A red and gold, and red and gold, and red and gold again striped tent, with black cords tying the flaps apart and posters on cane poles.

There is a job for Peter Richardson a job for Susan Wong, a job for Pamula Robeson and a job for Daniel Ayes, a job like no other job in a project like no other project, "Project Romulus" the renaissance of the wolf.

"Come on up, come one come all, take the punt, take the boat, take the flight to the apple isle."

Nobody in the Society of the Wolf did.

Henk Van Der Sarr did not expect them to, not on day one, not on day two or three, but a little and a little more he knew he would convince the best and the brightest to devote their enviable enthusiasm to his project, to his vision of the future of the wolf. Meanwhile the dam would continue, the water would rise higher and their options sink lower against the shore of his dam.

Even before the Mersey Pondage had reached the height of one metre lapping the barricades and swamping the tents of the Society of the Wolf, Nat knew he alone had the technology to thaw Henk Van Der Sarrs plans. To wreak revenge on the society which has stolen his hero, and to undo, all which they had failed to undo by pressing the button marked U.

He has an invention; Invention 29B.

Naturally he hasn't built it yet, except in a scale version he'd slung from the ceiling of his bedroom and controlled from the bed-head with fine fishing twine. This prototype version flew for approximately six seconds. It might be enough.

Invention twenty nine B is a dam-buster. Modelled on the famous Lancaster Dambuster squadron and consisting of a wicker ladder fuselage suspended via a series of slings to a number four climbing rope, a double abseils and carrying a round drum-like bomb in its belly.

Nat and Rosalind lay on his bed, beneath the Messerschmitt's of Nat Klein's childhood, supposedly discussing this project. Rosalind is not being serious. Nat realized this when Rosalind raised her blue lambs-wool sweater, when she unbuttoned her white cotton tunic and shirt, and asked him to kiss me, please kiss me, on one and another taut, dark nipples. And now a little further, let my dress fall below me, let Nat lay beneath me, so I may gently rock, desire upon desire. For the body is a landscape whose contours are oh so unquenchable.

Nat also realized his great uncle would recall the exact specifications, the size of the payload, and most importantly for the purposes on invention twenty-nine B, the mechanics by which the cylindrical bomb was released, the air speed, the height, all the detail he would need to knock out this dam from his crevasse ladder Lancaster. His uncle would know, all Nat wished to know and more. If he were speaking to his uncle, he could ask him. Except he was not.

Nat was thinking of the payload release as Rosalind raised a blue lambs-wool sweater, he was thinking of the wind speed as she unbuttoned a white cotton tunic and shirt, but he was thinking only of Rosalind as he kissed one, then another dark nipple. He was thinking he loved her.

Nat Klein sent on the evening of September the thirteenth a set of questions to his uncle. Questions of vectors, questions of force, questions of trajectories graphically displayed just how his uncle would have drawn them. He sent them on a Society of the Wolf postcard borrowed from Mary, who Rosalind was speaking to. He sent it via the Museum's internal mail system to a room one door away and awaited a reply.

On Wednesday Rosalind Son-Lee sat in the pilot seat wearing the leather flying cap and goggles while Nat connects a crevasse ladder to the underbelly of her seat.

"Never, never, never, Nat," says Rosalind, "Will I again be your test pilot, no matter how necessary, no matter how just."

On Wednesday, ten hours before Rosalind sat in the pilot's seat the *Melbourne Age* printed the first advertisement, for the first rally, to Save the South West Wing. Stan "Scoop" Munro called Di Jacobson, Di Jacobson called the society and the society called to order. "It is a time for action," the President proclaimed, "a time to honour our dedication to Mersey Camp, to the Tiers beyond, to those who have gone before and those who struggle now, the incomparable Green Avenger, to ourselves, our friends, our fraternity, it is a time for action a time to fight."

A time to revive the pageant, this Saturday coming on the steps of the Victorian Museum, to retrieve puppets badly bruised and sodden from the framework of the barricades, now submerged beneath the rising level of Mersey Camp pondage and preform again, a parred down pageant in the bare space of the Museum steps in an uneasy wind of a September Saturday.

Susan Wong wore the wolf suit, Peter Richardson played piccolo, Samantha and Sue held the poles of the birds in motion, Max Roland played on congos, Jack Rivers pulled the antechinus strings and Jeremy Rivers was the Tasmanian Devil. Many amongst the crowd wore, "No Dams!" T-shirts, many others wore Society of the Wolf T-shirts. The crowd both a demonstration and an audience to a procession of egrets, their crescent plumage rustling, thrill feathers in a thrill wind.

Susan Wong as the Tiger Wolf snarled loud and snarled long but neither long enough nor loud enough to reverse the swelling of the water around Mersey Camp, the course of the steamer Singapore bound on a pastel blue sea, the construction in a Hobart warehouse of seventeen, seven by four meter prefabricated modules soon to be transported to lake Salome shores, or even the momentum of a crevasse ladder Lancaster dam buster on a number four sling following the trajectory from roof beam to pond. However veraciously, however raucously Susan Wong brayed nothing at all, reversed tail and beat it.

Susan Wong, alone amongst the Society recognized that, Susan Wong alone had met, confidentially in the Museum coffee shop, Tony Paxton Environmental Liaison Officer, H.E.C. They spoke candidly.

Of the wolf, "Only Henk Van Der Sarr can save the wolf, only he has the resources."

Of the snow-jar, "The snow-jar is just a model, Project Romulus is reality."

Of the future, "We are the future."

While Susan Wong brayed, and the pageant marched. Mary Becket sold thirty-seven "No Dams!" T-shirts. Thirty-five was the number she had been waiting two months, eleven days, seventeen hours and six minutes to reach. Thirty-five was her ticket to Helsinki. "Zoey Dearest," he wrote, "Today at one twenty-seven Melbourne time I sold the T-shirt which will propeller me across the continent of Eurasia, I sold it to a nondescript man in a grey woollen suit who said he liked to support every day in whatever way the dying embers of capitalism. That was not, I answered, strictly speaking the point. Wasn't it, he winked the most fragrant of winks. Mersey Camp is sinking slowly beneath the malevolence of Great Western Tasmanian rain. The Society, standing firm against the H.E.C., Museum Security, the Subcommittee in charge of exhibitions and elements of hostility from Anita Craig's tours. Di Jacobsen did so want to be president of something. Dearest Eugene continues to imagine lands, no longer where the wolf once roamed, but the land where Nadia, his romantic Nadia voyages through a landscape of his dreaming. My dream is when he finds her, in a place with a name like Lipnik, with many mountains dipped in snow, that when he goes there, arriving early morning on the Vienna Express he will find not Nadia but Mary O'Becket, wouldn't that be a glorious way to meet. Why Zoey, why, why, why, do we want them so?"

43. Boom!

Once again Rosalind sits with a certainty of calamity in the pilot's seat of Nat's crevasse ladder Lancaster, wearing the leather pilot's cap and goggles while Nat adjusts an intricate assembly of levers, pulleys and gears which in the machines heart shift lead weights along the belly of the fuselage.

"Pull the yellow lever thirty degrees towards you."

Nat adjusts the tilt, wing tip to wing tip.

"And the red lever thirty degrees away."

Yes, it dipped delightfully.

"And now the red lever towards you and the yellow away."

The nose lifted, the tail dropped, the starboard wing dipped, and the port rose in an elegant imitation on a banking Lancaster.

"It's almost ready for the bomb."

And oh, what a bomb.

What a glorious, glorious bomb, a cylindrical, red, white, and blue bomb with B.O.M.B. written in black lettering and a star on both circular ends. The bomb which Nat painted Rosalind filled with cochineal and phosphorous. The bomb that Rosalind filled with cochineal and phosphorous, Nat fixed to the belly of the bomber following the diagram coaxed from his uncle. A diagram drawn on sheets of green graph paper, numbered one to forty-two, including part twenty-seven A, screw, clockwise turning, A/F one sixteenth thread, part fifteen, gear wheel, twelve centimetres diameter, part sixteen, gear wheel, five centimetres diameter, part seventeen, linked chain. In the seven pages of instruction not one mention of the speed of rotation or height from which the bomb should fall, or how, if at all, they are related.

It is too late for technicalities, it is time for the bomb, on Saturday morning when the pageant begins.

When the pageant began, impishly on piccolo, meditatively of clarinet, the high-water mark of the Society membership peaked simultaneously with the high-water mark of Mersey Camp dam. The first at four hundred and eleven, the second at one point two five meters, a level which laps the pandanus on the walk-way rising up, and reduces the clearance, Lancaster to water to seventy-two centimetres, reducing the possible payload to fifty-five kilograms. Nat calculates, the crevasse ladder Lancaster at seven kilograms, the bomb at two, leaving forty-six for the pilot, exactly the weight of Rosalind Son-Lee in leather pilot's jacket, leather cap and goggles.

But even in the afternoon of September the twenty fifth as they assemble the Lancaster between the black poly-pipes on the dark side of the dome, Rosalind is still reluctant to fly it. As the pageant circles to an up-tempo waltz between the columns of the Museum entrance, the Lancaster rises on double-four nylon over the lip of the snow-jar. Rosalind has acquiesced, but only if she can wear Nat's beloved black silk scarf of the Green Avenger, the insignia and the mantra of the hero.

As the wolf bays its way through the crowd assembled, Rosalind Son-Lee reaches her ceiling, two meters below the Museum roof, she tilts the Lancaster nose downwards, adjusts her balance, wing tip to wing tip, and gently eases into the descent.

As Di Jacobson wearing an identical cloak and mantra of the hero begins to whistle the wolf sutra while recognizing that amongst the puppetry and pandemonium that this is the first time she has been happy in a decade. Rosalind Son-Lee plummets towards the bottom of her trajectory, releasing two kilograms of phosphorus and cochineal onto the still waters of Mersey Camp dam.

In the pink explosion which followed, Rosalind Son-Lee catapulted fifteen meters into the air, broke an arm, bruised her rip cage and scorched the first three centimetres of hair from her forehead. Rosalind Son-Lee would forgive Nat Klein for her left arm, for her rip cage, but never for scorching her black fringe away.

In the pink tide of flood-water which followed the pink explosion, were washed away, the recruitment tent of the H.E.C., all the partitions, all the photos, all the maps, and the entire vision of the Hydro Electricity Commission, and all the dreams of the Society of the Wolf.

PART 7.

By The End of;

Hobart Mercury
A New Future for the Walls of Jerusalem

The Lake Sidon project will bring the Walls of Jerusalem National Park into the twenty irst Century, complete with ive-star accommodation and a heliport adjacent to Hall's Island. No longer will the wilderness area be the exclusive domain of intrepid walkers, the project will open The Walls of Jerusalem to world tourism.

"A unique development," says a spokesperson for the Tasmanian Premier, exactly the sort of project the Island State need. When asked if he expected opposition from the conservationists the spokesman replied, "I think we are well and truly over those dark days."

44. By the End of,

By the end of the year of the white-wolf Martin McKenzie stood on Mount Ophel escarpment, the wind blowing South by South West, twenty-five knots, the temperature, twelve degrees celsius {out of the wind}, a chill plus four within it. Henk Van Der Sarr had brought him here, to introduce him to a most wonderful idea. The idea's name is ice. A canvas of ice, not curtailed by the boundaries of a snow-jar, by the narrowness of a vision conceived in another century, or by the cheerless men who sit on sub-committees. "This," says Henk Van Der Sarr, sweeping a proprietary arm one hundred and eighty degrees across a landscape of escarpment and lake, "Is the place for your poly-pipes."

Martin McKenzie trails a two-hundred-meter tape measure from the tip of the escarpment up a rock screwn gradient, pegging a vast rectangle around the figure of Henk Van Der Sarr, who he returns to sit before, calculator in hand, dispensing forever with running a torch bulb, he asks for a hectare of coolers and he'll re-create a glacier. "Done," says Henk Van Der Sarr with astonishing speed, before their voices are drowned out by choppers.

All morning through the Gate of the Chain the helicopters have chuu-chuu, chuu-chuu, choppered, entering and exiting the Lake Salome site, parting Hobart with pre-fab puzzles rotated until an edge finds an edge as block by block the yellow moulded spine of the modules rise. Module one, completed in the first week of December houses the laboratories of Project Romulus, the quarters of Jacky Lambert Project Leader Lake Salome base.

"A remarkable outcome from watching arctic wolves from a Piper Chero-kee, don't you think?" she asks Martin McKenzie as they discuss the laying of poly-pipe and polystyrene in the southern gullies of Mount Ophel and Zion. "The world," he replies, "Is ruled by chance." As he calculates to one thou-sandth of a degree the kinds of temperatures, he will need to build a glacier.

By the end of the year of the white-wolf the Society dedicated to its pres-ervation gathered from the cochineal debris of Mersey Camp, pink tents and scorched bedding and quietly, inconspicuously, slipped away. Di Jacobson to become a radio commentator on Melbourne Community Radio's "Vanishing Planet Hour". Peter Richardson, on piccolo, Max Roland, on Congo's to join with Jeremy Klein in forming the group "Indigenous Jazz". And Susan Wong joined Jacky Lambert in Module two of Lake Salome camp.

By the end of the year of the white-wolf Rosalind Son-Lee's fringe had re-grown with a pink triangle on the crown of her head. She wasn't going to see Nat so much anymore, and she wouldn't have, "no way", if only she could wish that silly girl part of herself away. And if Nat hadn't found the camera, a second hand standard eight-millimetre movie camera which belonged to Mary O'Becket.

"You could do something wonderful with this." she said, and he knew immediately he unwrapped it, she was right.

The first thing Nat Klein filmed on standard eight film were the maned wolves at Melbourne Zoo. He told Rosalind, as he told everybody, "Film will be the fossils of the twenty first century". Surprisingly Rosalind Son-Lee agreed and just as surprisingly agreed again to become his scientific adviser.

By the end of the year of the white-wolf Eugene Klein stood in the depar-ture lounge, Melbourne airport, kissing Mary a longing farewell, before her QANTAS 747 departed for Munich. Things change but not much, thirty-nine years ago he kissed Nadia a heart-breaking farewell on a nondescript train station in the English midlands. The departure lounge is clean, the departure lounge isn't blacked out, there are no infantry men sleeping on the benches, but the heart cares little for the update. The yearning is the same. What can he say, he asks her to write and she did.

45. "Follow Them!"

The first letter, a *Thylacine alpina* postcard posted in Munich, related a story which astonished him. A story of a journey, a caravan moving between the cities of central Europe, two Thylacines, curiosities of a distant continent, paraded before the European crowds, under the auspices and advertising the existence of, a unique wilderness experience on the Great Western Tiers, "Project Romulus" one Lufthansa flight away. Eugene Klein placed this postcard into the expanding map of the dream. He places it in the white side, however curious, however bizarre, however dreamlike its message. On a Society of the Wolf postcard he scrawls a two-word message, "Follow them."

"Zoey Dearest," Mary writes, "I'm here, can you believe it I'm actually here, I can't believe it. It is much more crowded and much more frantic and much more more-ish than anything I expected. And you won't believe what else, the Thylacines have followed me, or I have followed them. This is good, this is better that I ever could have dreamed. This is the bait and I am the hook and Gene, my Gene, will come running. Do you think he'll come running? For the Thylacines? For me? He'd be crazy if he didn't."

From the moment Mary O'Beckets flight disappeared into the mauve evening Melbourne sky Eugene Klein had decided that she would not write and that he would not follow. Simply because he was wrong about her writing didn't mean he was wrong not to follow. He hadn't followed Nadia when the war was over, and Mary, however much one longing resembles another, is not Nadia, and Eugene is so much older and so less certain, of his place, in her journey, in her heart, to live at the whim of her private I-Ching.

Once again, in the absence of courage Eugene hesitates.
On the Salzburg, Vienna express Mary O'Becket orders a long black coffee from an impatient waiter in a black dress suit and sits in the dining carriage Eugene dreamed of. She scribbles on the back of an "I love Wolf-gang" postcard, "Henk Van Der Sarr is here." and addressing it to Eugene, while she waits for her order.

The man in compartment twenty-seven A, the man on the platform of the Salzburg station certainly looked like Henk Van Der Sarr. Mary O'Becket positioned herself where she could watch every person who entered, every person who left the dining carriage on the Vienna express, the last seat on the starboard side, {is it starboard on trains} naturally it is the seat occupied by Eugene in the dream, and for, no doubt, the same reason.

She reads the European edition of the *Guardian*, in which there is an advertisement detailing membership of "Project Romulus, the renaissance of the wolf." There are three grades of membership, the student, the supporter and the sponsorship, as there was in her society. She clips it out of the news-paper and will attach it to the note she will send Eugene from Vienna.

"Vienna, October twenty seven, morning," Mary O'Becket sits in the cafe 'Flora' under palms which belong on the St. Kilda esplanade, writing a note to Eugene, "The circus has arrived complete with big top tent striped green and white, and yellow around the trim, with Thylacine videos, with Thyla-cine masks, with a perfect miniature replica of our dear snow-jar howling blizzards and crusting ice, and a T-shirt franchise the envy of my barrow."

"Henk Van Der Sarr, for it was Henk Van Der Sarr is in Vienna, holed up in the Hotel Tiga and not taking messages. I saw him on the Rotenturm-strasse and I saw him in the Volksgarten, I waved to him, he didn't wave back. I have sent him a postcard, a Society of the Wolf postcard on it I wrote the message, "Let then go free". And signed it, a friend. I am my darling," she concluded, "In pursuit."

Eugene received the letter on Armistice Day in the year of the white wolf. The night before the letter, he dreamt the dream again.

The dream has changed. Eugene did not notice the dream had changed while he sat at the table waiting for his coffee. He did not notice the dream had changed, during the moment in the dream when he first saw Nadia, arguing with the short, dark haired man at the opposite end of the carriage, nor did he notice that the dream had changed when he passed the long siding, the hamlet or the gorge spanning bridge. The moment Eugene noticed the dream had changed was the moment Nadia turned and looked towards him. The dream had changed because it was no longer Nadia. It was Mary.

Mary O'Becket travelled Vienna to Prague on November the tenth arriv-ing Hlavni station at three fifteen. Henk Van Der Sarr was undeniably on this train, she did not see him. The *Thylacine alpinas* were undeniably on this train, she did not find them. She looked. She walked through every carriage, poked her head in every compartment which wasn't locked, seven were locked, sat both ends of the dining car, tried {unsuccessfully} to smile her way into the baggage sections on the pretext of finding her winter coat. "I didn't realize how cold it would be in Prague" translated into Chek with the expression, "Brrrr."

She had to admit, and she wrote as much to Eugene, that espionage is more Nat's caper than hers.

Eugene return reply, picked up in *Poste Restante* Prague was naturally one letter out of synch. It asked her to pursue, which she is. It asked her to supply the itinerary of the wolf, which she hasn't. And to tell her, even after a week he has begun to miss her.

She misses him too. She tells him so. In the letter he will receive on November twenty one. The letter which includes the itinerary, Breslin, Katowice, Krakow {Zakopane}, Warsaw, Berlin, Leipzig. Eugene Klein underlined the town Krakow, the excursion to Zakopane in red texta. Pinned the letter to the top right-hand corner of his vast memorabilia map and in the same red texta drew a line from the letter to the top right-hand corner to the letter in the bottom left hand corner, a startling red line with the words, "the wolves are going home" written upon it.

He wrote immediately to Mary.

He sent her a map. An exquisitely detailed espionage map. He drew the interior of the compartment correct down to the cracked hot water faucet. Mary hadn't doubted that he would, the moment she saw the snow daubed mountains she knew she had entered the dream. The map, the map of the dream, and she its heroine.

Mary O'Becket glanced at Mary O'Becket in the mirror of compartment eleven A, dressed in the vampish dress, stiletto heels of Eugene's imagination. "These are," Mary says to herself of the stilettos, "Like trying to walk on ice-skates."

The journey from compartment eleven A to dining car is drawn in black footstep shadows on Eugene Klein's map. The train's position in the world relative to Marys position in the aisle is illustrated with tiny cross-section miniatures of the north bound train, such that the map exists simultaneously as a map and as a narrative.

The map is the landscape of Joseph's nostalgia, the narrative a story of romance and adventure, just as it ought to be, just as Nat would have willed it, just as Nat would have drawn it.

Mary O'Becket enters the dining car as the train passes the forest which begins the dream. The forest is dark; in the dream it is snowing, noiseless white blotches against the windows, outside the train, it is snowing identical blotches. As Mary approaches Henk Van Der Sarr she smiles the smile which reminded Eugene of a sparkler.

She asks, as she passes, "Excuse me, but do you speak English," and gushes, "That's such a relief," when he nods, "Yes," he does.

"May I?" she asks, sitting beside him, "I didn't know how much I'd miss my mother tongue."

"English is my second tongue."

"I'd never know." she laughed, and he smiled at the obvious lie.

"You are being," Henk Van Der Sarr observes correctly, pointedly, "glib."

"It's a glib world."

"So, what are you doing in this glib world?"

"Seeking the man who stole the Thylacines."

"If you find him, what will you do?"

"Ask him to free them."

"Perhaps the man, who you say, has the Thylacines would like, would dearly like, for there to be a land where the Thylacines could be free. And perhaps when he returns that land to how it was he shall return the Thylacines to it. And perhaps my friend from the Society of the Wolf would better serve them by assisting in the restoration of the Tiers rather than writing postcards to strangers."

Mary stared at this audacious man, who does he think he is? She thought, who does he bloody well think, he is? She wanted to say something venomous and awful, she wanted to say something to cut through his arrogance, but all she could think of saying at that moment was to ask very simply.

"Can I see them?"

Henk Van Der Sarr passed Mary Becket a free pass to the circus called, "Project Romulus" and said with the most tart of smiles, "If you like."

This is the moment in the dream and the instant in the present when the heroine parts angrily from the short spectacled man. This is the moment when the train crosses the steel latticed bridge, bank to bank, of a deep pine green gorge. And this is the moment when Mary steps black stiletto footprint to black stiletto footprint along the aisle of the map, to find, as the train click clacks across Czechoslovakia , in the last or first seat of dining car B, Eugene Klein waiting for the coffee he has ordered.

46. The Dream continues.

On the ninth of December, in the end of the year of the white wolf, at eleven thirty-seven Eastern Standard Time, two thirty-seven Zakopane time, the dream continues.

It is snowing. The snow is falling in massive flurries, Eugene cannot see the locomotive and can barely see the caboose. He does not expect to see the locomotive which seventeen carriages in front of him, but the caboose is only three baggage carriages to the rear. They can see the last baggage carriage, they can see the vent. Eugene believes they can pry the vent open, if only they can reach it. The access ladder to the roof of the baggage cars is crusted in ice, the roof itself may be worse. Eugene is wearing his blue canvas climbing sac. He has removed a small Chamonix ice-axe which he uses to chip ice from the metal rungs. He clamps karabiners to the rungs above and breathes heavily to warm his fingers. Mary is shivering, brushing snow from her eye-brows, her forehead, her cheeks and says "Hurry" above the clatter of the train wheels clanging.

Eugene reaches the roof, he fixes a number four nylon rope to the top of the access ladder and begins roof vent to roof vent to traverse the roof ridge. Over this line Mary can follow, hesitantly, fearfully, saying to herself, "I know I can, I know I can." And she can, and can again across the second of three baggage cars. On the roof of the third they will stop to pry, with ice-axe and ice-hammer the largest vent from its rivets. The largest vent is a small window so tight, you can just squeeze through window, into which they lower the climbing sac, Mary O'Becket and finally Eugene.

There is no thump when the climbing sac lands, no thump when Mary lands and no thump at all when Eugene lands. When Eugene lands he realizes why. They have landed on snow.

"What the heck?" says Eugene as he takes Mary's hand, noticing through the mist, the tents of ghosts with the mysterious message, "Let them run free," daubed in lipstick on their vestibule flaps.

It is the camp of ghosts which inexplicitly appeared in the snow jar, the same long-ago camp of his memory where he glimpsed the white wolf on Lake Sidon shore. The lake is familiar, the inverted ice-cream cone tents are familiar, the pencil-pines, the escarpment ridges frosted with white cloud, all exactly as they placed them using a one to one scale.

God's scale; they never, ever should have used it. It cannot be trusted.

Eugene Klein asks himself, at this moment, in this time, does he truly want to alter the scale, to distil mystery, clarify myth and be in a world without the last whiff of magic. Or lie in a camp bed, in the camp of ghosts, with a very real Mary beside him.

Mary who touches Eugene's bare arms, Eugene's bare shoulders, Eugene's dark hair and dizzy with helium thoughts in her head, she smiles the smile of a sparkler, kisses him lightly on a snow crusted brow and whispers, "Today, I will see your famous white wolves."

In pre-dawn light of December ten, Eugene Klein wears the black linen cloak of the Green Avenger and whistles the tune of the sutra.

White mist,
White snow,
White Wolves running.

Out from the pines on Lake Sidon shores, out onto the snowbanks rippled by wind, a boy in a fur jacket watches them run, over the train tracks to a Lake Zakopane shore.

"Two wolves in the blue snow, I saw them today
Mum."

www.ingramcontent.com/pod-product-compliance
Lightning Source LLC
Chambersburg PA
CBHW031207260626
47169CB00004B/1283